SUMMER AT WILLOWCREEK STABLES (A HEALING HORSE STORY; SHOW JUMPING FICTION)

A WILLOWCREEK NOVEL OF HORSES, HOPE, AND QUIET STRENGTH

(THE WILLOW CREEK SEASONS)
BOOK THREE

LAURA ASHWOOD

CONTENTS

EPILOGUE

The last ribbons of the spring show fluttered in the late daylight as Clara Bennett walked with Aspen along the quiet path behind Willowcreek Stables. The crowds had faded. The music from the loudspeakers had been silenced. Only the soft rustle of leaves along the creek and the rhythmic fall of Aspen's hooves against the sand remained. Clara let her fingers run through his mane, feeling the warmth of him, the solid rise and fall of his breath that had anchored her through the most difficult months of her life.

Second place. Not perfect. Not flashy. But absolutely her own.

She had ridden without fear. She had chosen courage over expectation. She had stood up to Victor Hale without apology. And she had walked away without anything but the certainty that she had done what was right for herself and her horse. The thought brought a quiet, satisfied smile.

Luke had met her outside the ring after her ride. No lectures, no analysis, just that steady look that told her he understood everything she had said without needing words. He had placed a hand on

Aspen's neck, then on her shoulder, and nodded once. It had been enough.

Now the barns behind her glowed with golden evening light. A cluster of riders gathered near the notice board, pointing at the flyer for the upcoming summer medal circuit. The paper flapped gently in the breeze. Clara felt its tug, a reminder that the next challenge would not wait long.

A young man lingered among the riders, studying Aspen with a focused, measuring expression. She had noticed him earlier. Tall, dark hair falling across his forehead, posture too straight to be casual. His eyes had been sharp, as if he was memorising the length of Aspen's stride. When she had met his gaze, he had turned away without a word.

Knightfall's colours were stitched on the sleeve of his jacket.

Luke had mentioned that Knightfall had taken an interest in some of Willowcreek's riders. They had money, reputation, a training program that produced champions with alarming consistency. They liked to recruit quietly. Strategically. Looking for riders who were talented and impressionable. Clara hoped they were not planning to cause trouble, but the unease lingered.

Later that night, as the riders cleaned tack and rolled up bandages, a courier arrived with a single note addressed to Willowcreek: *We will be in touch.* No signature. No context. Only a crest stamped in deep blue wax. Knightfall Equestrian Center.

Clara had wanted to ignore it. She had wanted to pretend the world outside Willowcreek could wait while she reclaimed her peace. But summer crept forward relentlessly, filled with whispers of new riders, new rivalries, new tests of courage.

As she entered Aspen's pasture and unclipped his lead rope, he paused beside her. For a moment he simply breathed, warm and steady against her arm. Then he stepped away into the dimming evening, tail swishing, head high.

Clara watched him for a long time, and she understood something important. Spring had been about healing. Summer would be about rising.

And she would face it on her own terms.

She closed the gate, took a slow breath, and whispered into the violet air.

"Whatever comes next, I am ready."

1

Morning arrived with a glow that felt almost unreal. A warm curtain of sunlight stretched across Willowcreek Valley, spilling over rolling hills, shimmering along the surface of the slow moving creek, and settling like a soft blanket over the stables. Birdsong rose from the hedgerows. Dust motes floated lazily in the beams of light that slipped through the open doors of the indoor arena. Summer had not merely arrived. It had taken full possession of every inch of the barn.

Clara stood at the pasture fence with her arms folded on the top rail, watching Aspen graze in the golden half light. His chestnut coat had grown gleaming and rich with the season, catching the early sun as though he held it in his skin. His tail flicked rhythmically, relaxed and content. He lifted his head when he sensed her, ears pricked forward in greeting. It was the simple gesture that always made her chest tighten with affection.

"You look far too pleased with yourself this morning," Clara murmured as he walked toward her. "I know exactly why. You like summer a little too much."

Aspen halted at the fence and pressed his warm muzzle into her hand. The soft whiskers tickled her palm. Clara laughed quietly and leaned her forehead against his. His breath puffed gently, the familiar grounding sensation that always eased something inside her.

A faint breeze carried the smell of oiled leather, cut grass, and the unmistakable mix of sunscreen and fly spray that signaled show season. It also carried the chatter of riders gathering near the arena as they prepared for morning lessons. Their voices were excited, buzzing with plans for the medal circuit. Posters had appeared everywhere. On the tack room door. On the feed shed wall. On the refrigerator inside the lounge. Bright colours. Bold print. Prize money that made every teenager in the barn daydream more than they should.

Clara felt that buzzing excitement too. But it was softened by a small ripple of pressure she could not quite shake.

Spring had ended well. Better than she had ever dared to hope. Yet she could feel the new season pulling at her with expectations and whispered doubts. She had found courage again, but courage was not something that stayed still. It shifted. It changed. It needed tending like a young plant in a pot. Summer would test whether hers had roots strong enough to hold.

She stroked Aspen's forehead and smiled at him.

"New season. New challenges. Same us."

He nodded his head as if he agreed.

Behind her, the barn door slid open with a heavy rumble. Luke stepped into the morning light, rolling up the sleeves of his faded grey shirt. The sunlight caught in his hair and along the edge of the clipboard he carried under one arm. Clara could always tell when he was planning something. His steps held a certain purpose. Today was one of those mornings.

"Good. You are already out here," Luke said as he reached the fence beside her.

"I was watching him pretend to be majestic," Clara replied. "He is in a very dramatic mood today."

Aspen tossed his mane in confirmation, making both of them laugh.

Luke rested his elbows on the fence, matching her stance. He waited a moment, taking in the quiet scene of horse and rider in the soft morning air. Then he lifted the clipboard slightly.

"Medal season schedule," he said.

Clara groaned softly. "Please tell me it is not full of early mornings and rules that are impossible to read before breakfast."

"It is absolutely full of early mornings," Luke said, smiling. "But the rules are not impossible. Only unnecessarily detailed."

She took the clipboard from him. Papers clipped neatly together. The official rulebook printed with small text. Class descriptions. Scoring breakdowns. Sponsor listings. A full calendar of shows stretching from late June into early September.

Clara flipped through the pages, feeling her pulse rise a little.

This was real. The summer medal circuit. The thing every rider at Willowcreek had talked about since March. The thing she had always secretly wanted to try, even before the accident, even before fear had carved its space inside her. She was stronger now. More grounded. But this was a different level of pressure.

"What do you think?" Luke asked quietly.

"It looks... intense," she admitted. "But exciting."

"Do you want to try for it?" he asked.

Clara did not answer immediately. She watched Aspen wander a few steps away, swinging his tail through the warm air. His stride was light and springy, full of that summer energy she both loved and feared. She thought of the spring show. The nearly sabotaged jump. Her refusal of Victor Hale's contract. The sunrise ride that had changed everything for her.

Finally she nodded.

"I want to do it," she said. "But I want to do it the right way."

Luke studied her expression, then nodded once. "Good. Then we start preparing now."

He reached into his pocket and handed her a pen.

"Mark the shows you want to aim for. At least three before the semifinals. Enough to build confidence without burning you out."

Clara scanned the calendar. The first show was in two weeks. Willowcreek hosting the warm-up schooling day was in one week. She circled both. Then she circled a show in July, one in early August, and one mid-August.

"That should do it," she said.

"Ambitious," Luke replied. "But I think you can handle it."

The compliment warmed her. She handed him the clipboard.

"I will need a good training plan," Clara said. "Maybe a miracle or two."

"No miracles," Luke said. "Just consistency and trust. Aspen will do the rest."

Clara looked at her horse again. Aspen lifted his head and snorted as if he approved of this entire conversation.

"I think he agrees," she said.

"Knowing him, he would like extra treats added to the plan," Luke added.

They turned back toward the barn together. When they reached the doors, a group of riders came spilling out, talking rapidly. Lara, Jenna, and two of the younger girls hovered around a sheet of paper one of them held. Their expressions were a mix of excitement and alarm.

"Clara! Luke!" Jenna called. "Have you heard?"

"Heard what?" Luke asked.

The girls exchanged glances, then Lara held out the paper.

"A rumor is spreading that Knightfall wants to recruit one rider from Willowcreek this season."

Clara felt the words hit her chest like a dropped weight.

Knightfall. Again.

She tried to brush it off with a shrug. "It is just gossip."

"It is not," Jenna insisted. "My cousin rides at a barn near Knight-fall. She said they have been talking about expanding their youth program. They want someone with potential and momentum."

"Which could be anyone," Lara said. "They did not say a name."

"But Willowcreek is on their list," Jenna added. "Supposedly."

Clara forced her shoulders to relax. She tried to keep her expression calm.

"It does not matter," she said. "I am focusing on my own riding. That is all."

The girls exchanged curious looks, but they did not push further. They hurried toward the arena for warm up.

Luke lingered beside Clara. His expression stayed neutral, but she knew him well enough to see the concern behind his eyes.

"You alright?" he asked.

"Yes," she said quickly. Then softer, "It just caught me off guard."

She started walking toward the tack room, but Luke placed a hand lightly on her arm.

"Clara," he said quietly. "Listen to me. Knightfall can recruit whoever they want. You ride because you love it. You train because you choose to. No one owns your future but you."

The words sank deep. Clara nodded slowly.

"You are right."

"Of course," Luke said. "I usually am."

She laughed despite the knot in her stomach.

But as she saddled Aspen an hour later, the rumor lingered like a shadow across her thoughts. She brushed it away each time it returned, but it clung stubbornly.

Knightfall was not done with Willowcreek. Of course they were not. They had watched Aspen at the spring show. Someone had delivered that note. Someone had spoken her name with interest.

Whatever this summer would bring, it had already begun working beneath the surface.

Clara tightened Aspen's girth, checked the bridle, and stepped out into the hot, bright morning.

A long season stretched ahead. Ribbons and rivalries. Tests of heart and strength. New faces. New challenges.

She took a deep breath, placed her foot in the stirrup, and swung into the saddle.

"Alright," she whispered to Aspen as they walked toward the ring. "Let us begin."

And summer rose around her like a curtain lifting on a new scene, bright and daunting and full of promise.

2

A heavy sky pressed over Willowcreek Stables by the time the riders gathered for the afternoon clinic. All morning, the air had been thick with humidity, clinging to skin and tack like a damp curtain. Now the clouds built dark and swollen above the valley, ready to break open with the first crack of thunder. Horses tossed their heads and shifted their weight uneasily, sensing the change long before the riders admitted that the weather was turning.

Clara stood at Aspen's stall with a curry brush in hand, listening to the distant rumble. The storm had been forming since sunrise. She had hoped it might hold off until evening, but the sky had its own schedule, and it matched the tension inside her far too well. She brushed Aspen's flank in slow circles, trying to keep her own heartbeat steady. He responded with a soft snort and a flick of his ear. His muscles twitched beneath her touch, alert and restless.

"You hear it too," Clara murmured. "You always do."

The storm was not the reason her stomach felt tight, though it did not help. Today was the preview for the joint clinic between Willowcreek and Knightfall. Luke had been preparing riders all week, adjusting schedules, tweaking routines, and repeating reminders about focus and professionalism. Clara had listened carefully. She wanted to show up strong. She wanted to prove spring had not been a fluke and that she could carry her courage into summer.

Still, the thought of Knightfall riders watching her made her chest feel small.

The barn door creaked open, letting in a gust of warm wind that carried the first drops of rain. The riders looked up. Clara turned to see two figures stepping inside.

The first was Coach Amber Leigh, who had trained at Knightfall for years. She walked with quick, efficient steps, her expression sharp and unreadable. She carried a clipboard under her arm and wore a pale blue jacket with the Knightfall crest on the sleeve. Her presence alone made every rider straighten their posture a little.

The second figure followed her closely. Clara had never seen him before, but she recognised him immediately from the spring show. The boy with the dark hair who had watched Aspen with a cool, calculated gaze. He stood tall and relaxed, shoulders loose but held with a kind of contained power. He wore a black riding shirt tucked neatly into white breeches, and he moved in a way that suggested a lifetime of serious training.

Liam Carter.

Knightfall's rising star.

Clara felt Aspen lift his head behind her, ears snapping forward. His body tensed slightly, sensing the unfamiliar horse approaching outside. A high pitched trill of a neigh followed, sharp and commanding. Clara stepped to Aspen's shoulder and placed one hand gently on his neck.

"Easy," she whispered.

The tall black stallion that entered the barn made even seasoned riders blink. His coat gleamed like wet ink despite the gathering storm. His neck arched proudly as he surveyed the space, nostrils flaring as he snorted at the unfamiliar scents. His mane fell in thick waves to one side. He was stunning, powerful, alert, and unmistakably difficult.

Knightfall.

Clara had seen horses like him only in magazines and online show clips. Seeing him up close was a different experience entirely. He looked like he expected the world to stay out of his way.

Liam held the lead rope lightly, one hand resting just below the stallion's cheek. Knightfall responded to his touch with a slight tilt of the head, almost imperceptible, but enough to show the connection between them.

Luke appeared from the tack room, wiping his hands on a cloth. He approached Coach Amber with a polite smile.

"Welcome. Storm is rolling in faster than expected, but we will make do."

"We always do," Amber replied. She glanced around the barn, eyes lingering on each rider in turn. When her gaze passed over Clara, it paused only for a moment before moving on. Clara was not sure if that was better or worse.

Liam stood beside Amber, silent but observant. When he noticed Clara watching him, he met her eyes with a completely blank expression. Not unfriendly, not hostile, but impossible to read.

Clara looked away quickly and focused on saddling Aspen. Her hands felt clumsy. She forced herself to breathe slowly and keep her movements gentle. Aspen watched the stallion with wide eyes, stepping sideways once before settling again.

"He is just a horse," Clara whispered to herself. "A loud one. But still a horse."

Thunder growled overhead, closer now. Rain tapped against the roof in short bursts. The clinic would have to take place in the indoor arena. Good footing, but the echo of storms always made the horses edgy.

Luke approached Clara's stall as she tightened Aspen's girth.

"Storm or no storm, you will be fine," Luke said calmly. "Focus on your ride, not everyone else's."

"I am trying," Clara replied. "He looks like something out of a movie."

"Knightfall?" Luke smiled slightly. "He knows he is beautiful. That is half his trouble."

"And Liam?" Clara asked before she could stop herself.

Luke folded his arms. "Talented. Precise. Competitive. He comes from a long line of show riders. He is used to being the best in any ring he enters."

Clara swallowed. "Great."

"You do not need to compare yourself to him," Luke added. "Ride your horse the way you know best. Aspen responds to connection, not pressure."

Clara nodded. Aspen flicked an ear toward Luke, then pressed his nose gently into Clara's back. It grounded her.

"Alright," she said softly. "Let us do this."

They walked toward the indoor arena together. The storm darkened the light outside, casting long shadows along the barn aisle. The sound of wind grew louder, pushing against the siding with occasional rattles. The riders gathered near the arena entrance, waiting for Amber and Liam to join them.

When the pair entered, Knightfall let out a loud, trumpeting snort that echoed across the rafters. Aspen's head shot up, muscles tightening. Clara steadied him with a hand.

"Easy boy. You are alright."

Liam glanced over, taking in Aspen's reaction with a small, unreadable smirk. He leaned down and murmured something into Knightfall's ear. The stallion snorted again, pawing the ground.

Amber clapped sharply. "Riders, we will begin with a warm up on the flat. Keep distance, especially around the stallion. He will give a warning before he kicks, but I prefer not to test it."

A few riders laughed nervously. Clara did not. Aspen's ears shifted back and forth, unsettled.

As they mounted, the wind outside picked up, dragging a low moan along the roof. The first flash of lightning lit the indoor arena in a white burst. Aspen stiffened beneath Clara, but she stayed calm, settling deeper in the saddle.

"It is alright," she murmured.

Liam mounted Knightfall with the ease of someone who had been doing it since childhood. He adjusted his reins, signaled with a slight pressure of his leg, and the stallion lifted into a collected walk, fluid and powerful.

The riders began circling. Amber observed closely, arms crossed, her gaze sharp as she took notes. Luke watched from the opposite side, staying out of Knightfall's path.

Clara kept Aspen on the outer rail, giving Knightfall a wide berth. The stallion eyed them each time they passed, ears pricked, neck arched as if challenging Aspen silently. Aspen responded by raising his head too high and quickening his pace.

"Stay with me," Clara said softly, lowering her hands and breathing slowly. She felt his back muscles soften, but tension still clung to him.

Liam guided Knightfall through a trot transition that was so precise it looked effortless. The stallion floated, hooves barely whispering on the sand. Clara could not help but watch for a moment, almost mesmerised.

"Eyes up," Luke called from across the ring. "Ride your horse."

Clara straightened immediately and focused on Aspen again. She gave him a soft inside leg, asked for a bend, and felt him relax slightly around her leg.

"Better," Luke said.

Amber walked toward Clara, watching her carefully.

"Your horse is sensitive," Amber said. "Good for feel. Bad for pressure. You must keep your core steady and your hands elastic, or he will lose rhythm."

Clara nodded. "Yes. I know. He needs confidence from me."

"Then give it," Amber said. "Every stride."

She moved on without waiting for a reply.

Clara swallowed her nerves. She worked on softening Aspen's

trot, finding a rhythm that felt like a shared breath. Slowly, the tension in her shoulders eased.

The storm outside intensified. Rain hammered the roof in sudden bursts. A crack of thunder shook the arena, and several horses flinched. Knightfall reared slightly, pawing at the air before Liam steadied him with calm hands.

"Show off," Clara muttered under her breath.

Aspen danced sideways, startled by the sudden movement of the stallion. Clara steadied him quickly.

Liam looked over, expression unreadable, and called across the arena.

"Your horse is reactive. Does he do that often?"

Clara exhaled through her nose. "Only when another horse behaves like a circus act."

Liam's lips twitched as if he found the answer amusing.

Amber clapped again. "Break into groups of three for jump warm ups."

Clara moved toward the center with Jenna and Lara. Liam joined Amber near the oxer being set. Megan Ward entered the arena at that moment, her timing impossibly perfect. She strode in with her helmet already buckled and Evermore polished to a shine. Evermore pranced as if announcing her arrival.

Clara's stomach tightened. Megan had not signed up for today's clinic.

Of course she came anyway.

Amber raised an eyebrow. "Late."

"I had training this morning," Megan said. "But I heard Knightfall might be scouting, so I thought I would drop in."

Clara felt her jaw tighten. Of course Megan heard the rumor.

Liam's gaze slid toward Megan with mild interest.

Amber shrugged. "Fine. Saddle up. Join group two."

Megan flashed Clara a thin smile before trotting away.

Clara forced herself to ignore her and focus on Aspen. She guided him toward the first warm up jump, a small cross rail. Aspen pricked his ears forward, eager despite the storm. She gave him a small squeeze and they lifted over it lightly. He landed soft and straight.

"Nice, Clara," Luke called. "Keep your leg steady."

Next was a small vertical. Clara approached with good rhythm, but Aspen hesitated slightly, distracted by Knightfall's loud snort across the ring. He jumped, but not smoothly. Clara stayed balanced but felt the wobble in his stride.

"Again," Amber said sharply, walking toward her. "Ride straight. Do not let other horses dictate his focus."

Clara nodded and circled back. She breathed deeply, softened her hands, and approached again. This time Aspen stayed in line and jumped with confidence. His landing felt like a soft cloud beneath her.

"Better," Amber said. "He has potential. But he is very sweet."

The way she said sweet made it sound like a flaw.

Clara guided Aspen forward when she heard Liam's voice from the far end of the arena. He spoke quietly, but the storm had quieted for just a moment, and his words travelled farther than he intended.

"He is sweet. But sweet horses rarely win medals. They do not have the drive for it."

Clara felt the words hit like a cold needle beneath her ribs.

Her hands tightened on the reins before she forced herself to loosen her grip. Aspen flicked an ear back toward her, sensing the shift in her heartbeat.

Not medal material.

The phrase echoed inside her like distant thunder.

She did not respond. Not out loud. But something inside her hardened with quiet determination.

Aspen turned his head slightly as if sensing it too.

Clara stroked his neck.

"Sweet is not a weakness," she whispered. "And neither are we."

But even as she said the words, a tiny splinter of doubt lodged deeper inside her.

One that would return at the worst possible moment later in the season.

———

The storm pressed harder against the arena as the clinic continued. The wind howled through the rafters with a lonely, rising whistle, and rain pounded the metal roof with such force that riders could feel the vibration through the saddle. Horses shifted uneasily, catching the nervous energy that pulsed through the space in quick, bright threads.

Clara tried to breathe steadily, but Liam's comment gnawed at her thoughts. Sweet but not medal material. It echoed in rhythm with the rain. Aspen sensed her tension and carried it in the tightness of his stride. His ears flicked back toward her with each quiet inhale she tried to steady.

Luke watched from the rail with narrowed eyes. Clara knew he had not missed the shift in Aspen's posture. Or the way Clara held her shoulders. But he did not interfere, trusting her to find her balance again.

Amber's sharp voice cut through the storm.

"Group three, take the line of verticals. Control your pace. Do not let the weather or other horses distract your rhythm."

Megan pushed Evermore into a smooth, floating canter and headed for the line without waiting for her group. Classic Megan. She approached the jumps as if surrounded by cameras. Evermore gathered himself neatly and lifted over the first vertical with a perfect bascule. His knees tucked high, his landing soft, his neck arched as if he knew he was being watched.

Megan flashed a satisfied smile as she landed the final jump and circled with a proud lift of her chin.

Clara tried to ignore the prickle of irritation crawling up her spine.

Amber nodded once. "Strong ride. But watch your inside hand. You lift it too much."

Megan's smile tightened as she nodded back.

Jenna and Lara took their turns next, each ride altered by the thunder outside. Their horses jumped well, but with tension rippling through their backs. Clara could see the fear in their horses' eyes each time lightning flickered against the roof panels.

Then Amber turned toward Clara.

"Your turn," she said. "Show me that rhythm you found earlier. Keep your hands soft. And remember what I told you. Your horse is sensitive, not weak. Ride like you believe he can do this."

Clara swallowed, then nudged Aspen forward. He moved into a canter with a nervous bounce, neck arched a little too tight. She steadied him with a soft half halt, letting her hands follow his movement. She focused on the line of jumps ahead, letting the thunder fade from her mind.

"You can do this," she whispered.

They reached the first vertical. Clara kept her eyes forward. Aspen lifted neatly, clearing it with a clean arc. He landed straight and bounced toward the next jump with more confidence. She felt his stride stretch. He was trying. He wanted to please her.

They approached the second vertical. Clara softened her inside rein and let Aspen find the spot. He lifted again, landing with enthusiasm.

"That is it," Clara murmured. "You have got this."

Rain exploded across the roof in a sudden roar.

Aspen jolted.

The third vertical rushed toward them faster than Clara expected. She steadied him, but his stride faltered. His ears pinned back. He hesitated.

Clara felt the hesitation like a sudden hole beneath her seat.

"Leg," she whispered, urging him forward.

Aspen jumped, but it was uneven. He scrambled on landing.

Clara stayed balanced, absorbing the lurch with instinct. She kept her voice gentle.

"You are alright. Just the storm. You are doing so well."

Amber's voice carried across the ring.

"Good correction. Keep going."

Clara nodded and took the last vertical. Aspen found his rhythm again and lifted cleanly. They cantered away from the line with better balance, and Clara stroked his neck.

"That was brave," she said.

Liam watched from the far side of the arena, his expression as flat as the storm clouds above. He made no comment. Just observed. Knightfall stood beside him, the stallion's nostrils flaring with each crash of thunder.

Amber approached Clara with a thoughtful look.

"He is more capable than he thinks he is," Amber said. "But he needs a leader who believes in him every stride. Do not let outside pressure shake you."

Clara nodded. "I understand."

"Good," Amber replied. "Because this season will test that more than anything else."

Before Clara could ask what she meant, Amber was already walking toward the oxer being set at the far end of the arena.

Liam stepped forward, running a hand along Knightfall's neck. He spoke with Amber in low tones, but when he faced the riders again, his attention settled on Clara.

"Your horse looks careful," he said. "He thinks a lot before he jumps."

"Thinking is not a flaw," Clara replied.

Liam shrugged. "It can slow you down in the medal ring."

Clara tightened her hold on the reins. "Maybe speed is not the only goal."

Liam tilted his head slightly, studying her.

"You want to win, do you not?"

Clara opened her mouth, but Megan's voice cut in before she could answer.

"Of course she wants to win," Megan said, guiding Evermore closer. "Everyone here does. That is why Knightfall is watching us."

Clara bit the inside of her cheek.

Liam did not react to Megan's attempt at charm. He simply turned away, adjusting Knightfall's girth.

Amber called the next exercise: a bending line that required precision, confidence, and a responsive horse.

Megan volunteered to go first. She rode the line with polished ease, her posture perfect as Evermore sliced through each turn. She landed smiling, tossing her hair in a way that made Clara roll her eyes.

Jenna and Lara followed, each with a few mistakes but overall solid rides.

Clara was preparing for her turn when Liam approached her.

"You might want to tighten your outside rein on the second turn," he said. "Your horse tends to drift."

Clara blinked. "You have barely seen us ride."

"I notice things," he replied simply.

Then he walked away.

Clara could not tell if he was being helpful or condescending. She guided Aspen into a canter and headed for the bending line. She approached the first vertical with a calm, steady rhythm.

The second turn came quickly. Clara tightened her outside rein just enough. Aspen stayed balanced and surged forward. His ears flicked in determination. He cleared the second jump cleanly.

"Good correction," Luke called.

Clara allowed a small smile. The third jump approached, slightly higher than the others. Aspen lifted with confidence and soared over it.

"Nice ride," Amber said.

Clara felt relief wash over her.

But it was short lived.

Knightfall chose that moment to scream, a piercing, trumpeting call that split through the air like a blade. Aspen startled mid stride, landing stiff and hollow. Clara steadied him quickly, but she felt his panic creep like static beneath her saddle.

Knightfall pawed at the ground, lunging sideways. Liam pulled him back with strong hands, jaw tight.

"Easy," he muttered. "I know. The storm. Calm down."

But the stallion's eyes were wide and shining white. He tossed his head violently and snorted.

Aspen trembled.

Clara stroked his neck, trying to soothe him. "It is alright. I am here."

Another thunderclap exploded overhead. Loud enough to rattle the rafters.

Aspen shot sideways, nearly unseating Clara.

She held her balance but felt her own fear spike with the movement.

Luke stepped closer. "Take a moment, Clara. Breathe with him."

She nodded and lowered her hands, letting Aspen regain his composure.

Liam watched silently, then said under his breath, "This is why sweet horses struggle in storms. They spook easily."

Clara whipped her head toward him.

"He is not spooking because he is sweet. He is spooking because your stallion is about to take down half the arena."

Liam raised an eyebrow. "Knightfall requires a strong environment."

Clara's patience snapped. "He requires everything to go his way."

Liam shrugged. "If you plan on the medal circuit, you will have to handle horses like him."

Megan chimed in, smiling sweetly at Liam. "Some riders just are not built for pressure."

Clara's hands tightened around the reins. Aspen responded with a nervous stomp.

Luke stepped forward immediately. "Megan. Enough."

Megan opened her mouth to protest, but Luke raised a hand and pointed her toward the far end of the arena.

"Take a walk break," he said. "Now."

Megan huffed but complied, guiding Evermore away.

Amber signaled for the next rider. The clinic continued, but Clara felt the weight of the storm settling into her bones.

She walked Aspen in a quiet circle, letting the rhythmic sway calm them both.

But as the riders reconvened for final remarks, she overheard Liam speaking to Amber again. His voice was lowered, but the storm had softened for a moment, letting the words carry.

"He is sweet. Sensitive. But horses like that struggle under pressure. They do not push through fear. They pull back. Not medal material."

Amber did not respond.

Clara felt the comment like a bruise forming beneath her ribs. Not external. Not visible. But painful all the same.

She gathered Aspen's reins and walked toward the exit without waiting for Amber's closing notes. She could not stand another second under Liam's cool, appraising eyes. She could not stand Megan's smirk. She could not stand the storm or the echoes of her own worry ringing inside her skull.

Outside, rain fell in heavy sheets. Clara led Aspen toward the barn with her shoulders tight. The sky flashed with pale fire, illuminating his wet lashes and frightened eyes. She stroked his neck as they hurried inside.

"You are enough," she whispered fiercely. "I am enough. We are enough."

Thunder rolled again.

Aspen shivered.

Clara pressed her forehead against his, trying to shield him from the storm and from the words that had shaken her more than she wanted to admit.

The door slid open behind her.

She turned.

Liam stood there, rain dripping from his dark hair, Knightfall held firmly at his side.

For a moment, the world seemed to stand still.

Then Liam spoke.

"Your horse will need more than kindness if you want to survive medal season."

Clara stared at him, her hands still resting on Aspen's trembling neck.

"We will see," she said quietly.

Liam's gaze flicked from her eyes to Aspen's tense flank.

"We will," he replied.

The storm rumbled overhead.

And the first seed of doubt took root, deep enough to return when Clara least expected it, later in the season, when Aspen would refuse a jump he had never feared before.

3

Heatwave and Hard Lessons

By the end of June the valley felt like it had been placed beneath a giant glass dome. Heat settled over Willowcreek and refused to move, trapping every breath, every sound, every smell. The air above the paddocks shimmered in soft waves. Dust clung to boots and jeans and the inside of throats. Horses stood in the shade with drooping eyelids, tails twitching lazily at flies that never seemed to tire.

Clara felt the heat before she even stepped out of the truck that morning. It wrapped around her like a heavy blanket, thick and close. The edges of the sky were pale and washed out, without a single cloud to soften the sun.

She wiped sweat from her forehead with the back of her hand and headed toward the barn. The sliding doors stood wide open, but the air inside was only slightly cooler. Fans hummed at the ends of the aisles, turning slowly and stirring up barely enough breeze to move a strand of hay.

Aspen stood in his stall with his head lowered, one hind leg resting. His chestnut coat, usually full of bright copper shine, looked slightly dull under the weight of the heat. His eyes followed Clara as she approached, gentle and a little tired.

"Morning, handsome," Clara said softly as she unlatched the door. "You look how I feel."

He lifted his head and nudged her shoulder, but his usual spark was missing. His ears flicked toward the sound of the fan, then back to her, as if he could not decide what bothered him more, the heat or the buzzing noise.

Clara stroked his neck and felt the faint dampness under his mane. Heat lay trapped against his skin.

"We will keep it light," she promised. "Just some grids. Luke wants us to stay sharp for the schooling show."

She tried to sound cheerful, but her stomach gave a small twist.

The schooling show was in two days. The first proper step on the path to the summer medal circuit. Luke had mapped out their training carefully, with days for grids, days for flatwork, one day each week for quiet hacking along the creek. On paper, it made sense. In the middle of a heatwave, it felt slightly impossible.

As she brushed Aspen, Liam's words from the clinic crept into her thoughts again.

Sweet. Sensitive. Not medal material.

He had not said the last part directly to her face, but she had heard it. The phrase had been lodged under her ribs ever since, like a stone she kept bumping against.

Clara worked the brush over Aspen's shoulder, a little faster than necessary. He shifted his weight and exhaled heavily through his nostrils.

"Sorry," she whispered, softening her touch. "I am just thinking too much."

Out in the main aisle, Megan's voice floated through the overheated air, bright and confident.

"Make sure you get the angle where we clear the oxer. That one felt perfect."

Clara tensed.

She stepped out of Aspen's stall in time to see Megan holding up her phone to show Lara a clip from the previous day's ride. Evermore flicked across the screen, shining even through the pixelated video. The bay gelding cleared a wide oxer in slow motion, Megan's posture textbook neat, her smile easy and confident.

"I am going to post it with the schooling show hashtag," Megan said. "Might as well build some hype. The more people watching my rounds, the better."

Lara nodded politely, but Clara saw how her friend's shoulders slumped ever so slightly as she handed the phone back.

Megan noticed Clara near Aspen's stall and gave a little wave.

"Morning," she said. "Are you riding today in this oven?"

"We have grid work," Clara replied. "Luke wants us sharp."

"Same," Megan said with a shrug. "Heat is part of the game. Shows do not cancel for a little sunshine."

Clara opened her mouth to mention that this was more than a little sunshine, but she stopped herself. There was no point. Megan looked perfectly at ease, not a hair out of place despite the humidity.

"I posted the Knightfall clinic clip last night," Megan added, tapping her phone. "The one where Evermore took the bending line. People are already commenting. One of the girls from Knightfall liked it. Probably Liam's group."

Clara swallowed. "Nice."

"You should put up more videos of Aspen," Megan continued. "People love a comeback story. Sweet horse, nervous rider, summer medal circuit. It would get views."

Clara felt her cheeks warm, and not just from the heat.

"We are not doing this for views," she said, then wondered if that sounded childish.

Megan smiled, not unkindly exactly, but with a glint that made Clara feel as if she had said something naive.

"Suit yourself," Megan replied. "Just do not be surprised if the judges and sponsors watch the riders they know before they notice the quiet ones."

She turned and walked away, boots clipping neatly on the concrete. Her phone was already raised as she framed another short training video of Evermore standing in his stall, ears pricked, glossy coat catching the light.

Clara took a slow breath and went back to Aspen.

She checked his legs, lifted his hooves, and ran her fingers carefully along his back. No signs of soreness, just a general heaviness in his muscles that matched the heaviness in the air.

"Grid work, then a long hose down," she promised him. "And maybe carrots in a bucket of icy water. You like that."

He flicked one ear back in what she decided to take as agreement.

By the time she had tacked him up and led him toward the arena, sweat already trickled down the back of her neck. Her shirt clung to her shoulder blades. The air in the indoor was worse, thick and close despite the fans turned to full speed.

Poles and standards had been dragged into position: a line of small verticals set in a neat grid, distances measured with Luke's precise stride. The exercise was simple, on paper. In this heat, it felt like a test of willpower.

"Keep your sessions shorter," Luke had said during the morning briefing. "Make them count. Good warm up, focused work, then finish. Watch your horses. If they feel lethargic or dull, it may be the heat, not attitude."

Clara had nodded seriously, repeating the instructions in her head.

Now, as she mounted, she did her best to follow them.

Aspen lifted into a walk with less enthusiasm than usual. His ears stayed tilted sideways, as if listening for any excuse to stop.

Clara nudged him gently. "Come on. Just a light ride."

They started with a long walk on a loose rein, circling the arena until both of them loosened slightly. Outside, the air shimmered above the gravel road. The distant trees at the edge of the property looked hazy, their outlines smudged by the heat.

In the far corner, Luke adjusted the final grid pole and stepped back, hands on his hips.

"Once you have warmed up your horses, we will trot through the grid," he called. "Let the jumps do the work. You are there to balance, not to fight."

Megan and Evermore trotted past, already in a working frame, ears sharp despite the temperature. Megan's back remained straight, her hands still and light. Even from across the arena, she looked as if she were riding in a commercial.

"Smile, Evermore," she murmured. "We are on camera later."

Clara pushed the thought away and focused on Aspen. She shortened the reins, asked for a trot, and felt him step into it reluctantly.

His trot lacked its usual spring. His strides were shorter, his back slightly stiff.

"Come on, boy," she encouraged. "Wake up a little."

He flicked one ear back at her voice but did not brighten much.

"Well, he looks thrilled," Jenna muttered from across the ring on her paint gelding. She gave Clara a sympathetic smile.

"Heat is not his favourite," Clara said. "He would rather nap under a tree until October."

"Same," Jenna replied. "Luke keeps reminding me that medal season does not care about my personal preferences."

They shared a tired laugh.

Amber and Liam were not here today, at least, which removed one layer of pressure. Still, Clara heard Liam's words in her mind as she circled again.

Sweet. Sensitive. Not medal material.

Was this what he meant? That under pressure, under uncomfortable weather, under the weight of expectations, horses like Aspen would simply decide they were done and shut down?

Clara frowned at the thought and nudged Aspen into a more active trot.

He responded by tossing his head once and then grudgingly

lengthening his stride. His breathing became louder, nostrils flaring slightly.

Clara hesitated.

"He is just being lazy," she told herself. "He needs a reminder that work does not stop because of the weather."

She closed her leg a little more firmly and tapped him once with her heel.

Aspen surged forward with a small, annoyed bounce, ears pinning for a moment before pricking forward again.

"Better," Clara said out loud, trying to ignore the flutter of doubt in her chest.

Luke watched them carefully as they passed.

"Check his breathing after a few more laps," he called. "Do not push through the heat without listening."

"Okay," Clara replied, guilt prickling at her neck.

For the next few minutes they worked on circles and transitions. Clara tried to sharpen Aspen's responses, asking for more energy and quicker reactions. He gave them, but each time he obeyed, she felt a faint resistance underneath. Not a refusal, not yet, but a question. Are you sure? In this heat?

Sweat darkened the base of his neck. Foam gathered in small patches where the reins rubbed. His sides moved a little faster with each breath.

Clara told herself he would settle once they started the grid. Sometimes he woke up more when he saw poles.

Luke waved them in.

"Alright, bring them in at a strong trot. Let the poles lift their feet, and stay centered. If anyone feels their horse losing power or interest, circle out and walk. This is not about proving who is toughest. It is about building coordination."

Megan went first, as usual. Evermore trotted through the line of low verticals like a metronome, rhythm perfect. His hooves tapped lightly between each jump, then lifted cleanly. Megan's position stayed balanced and still, eyes up, heels down.

Luke nodded. "Good. That is what we are aiming for."

Megan slowed to a walk and patted Evermore's neck, her smile easy.

Clara swallowed and guided Aspen toward the line.

"Just like we always do," she whispered. "Small jumps. Nothing scary."

She felt his ears flick toward the poles ahead, then flatten slightly as a wave of hot air drifted from the far end of the arena. He shook his head once, as if annoyed by flies.

They approached the first pole. Clara eased her hands and let the rhythm carry them. Aspen lifted his feet through the ground poles cleanly, but his trot felt heavy, as if he were slogging through shallow water.

"Leg," she reminded herself.

She closed her calves around his sides in a quiet, insistent squeeze.

He responded, but only a little.

They reached the first small cross rail. Aspen pushed off with less power than usual, but he made it over, landing with a flat stride. His ears flicked forward toward the next element. He lifted again, but a fraction of a second late.

Clara leaned forward just enough to stay with him, but a flicker of unease slid down her spine.

"Again," Luke called as they landed. "But give him more impulsion on the approach. He is dragging his feet."

Clara nodded, cheeks heating. She circled at the far end of the arena, gathering Aspen together.

"You heard him," she murmured. "More impulsion. We can do this."

She closed her leg firmly and gave a small cluck.

Aspen tossed his head, then obeyed, his trot sharpening a little. They headed into the grid again.

This time they entered with better energy. Aspen lifted more neatly over the first cross rail. His front hooves snapped up with more intention. His back end followed with a bit more push.

"Good boy," Clara breathed.

They cleared the second element with more ease. For a moment, it felt like the heat had faded and they were back in cool spring air, both of them in sync.

Then, as they approached the third part of the grid, a fly landed near Aspen's flank. He flicked his tail sharply. The movement coincided with Clara's leg aid, and he seemed to misinterpret her cue. His stride shortened without warning.

Clara felt the ground rush up sooner than it should have. Aspen jumped, but with awkward timing. His front hooves clipped the top rail. The pole rattled and fell, clattering beneath his hind legs.

Startled, Aspen landed crookedly and stumbled forward.

For a heartbeat, everything tilted.

Clara felt her balance slip sideways. The world narrowed to the sensation of her left stirrup sliding away and the arena floor coming closer.

She grabbed for his mane without thinking, fingers clenching in the thick hair. Her body pitched forward. Aspen lurched, tried to regain his footing, and in the scramble, his shoulder dropped.

Her heel banged against a pole on the ground. Her heart jumped to her throat.

Then, with a desperate push from his hindquarters, Aspen righted himself.

Clara landed hard back in the saddle. The jolt shot straight up her spine. She gasped, eyes wide.

For a moment she saw the winter accident all over again. The too sharp turn. The slick ground. The split second where gravity had stolen every choice from her.

Her vision blurred. The breath left her lungs in a painful rush.

Aspen blew sharply, eyes wide and whites showing. His sides heaved. His ears jammed backward, trembling.

Luke's voice cut through the roaring in her ears.

"Circle, Clara. Let him walk. Let yourself breathe."

She managed to steer Aspen into a shaky circle. Her hands trembled on the reins. Her legs felt like they had lost all strength.

Jenna's voice reached her from across the arena, quiet and worried.

"You alright?"

Clara could not answer just yet. Her throat was too tight.

She stroked Aspen's neck with a hand that shook. His coat was slick with sweat now, darker patches under the saddle and girth.

"I am sorry," she whispered. "I am so sorry. That was my fault."

It had happened so fast, but she knew she had chased him into the grid with more leg than he wanted to give. She had pushed because she wanted to prove he was not lazy. Because she wanted to prove Liam wrong. Because she had let her fear of being seen as weak outweigh what she knew about this horse in this heat.

Luke approached slowly, giving both of them time to settle before he came close enough to speak softly.

"Talk to me," he said.

Clara swallowed hard. "I pushed him when he was tired. I felt him slow, and instead of listening, I told myself he was being lazy. Then the fly, the pole, and suddenly we were... falling again."

Her voice broke on the last word.

Luke nodded, expression gentle.

"He caught you," he said. "You both recovered. That matters."

"It felt like the accident," Clara whispered. "For a second I thought we were going down."

"I know," Luke replied. "Your body remembered that fall. It will do that for a while. But you stayed with him. That is different."

He laid a hand on Aspen's neck, feeling the horse's racing heartbeat.

"He is overheated," Luke said quietly. "Look at his flanks."

Clara did. Aspen's sides moved quickly, faster than they should after such light work. Foam had built up more under the girth. His nostrils flared as he tried to pull air through the heavy, humid atmosphere.

"We are done for today," Luke said firmly. "Walk him out, then cool him. No more grids."

Guilt washed over Clara again.

"I should have noticed sooner," she said. "You told us to listen to them. I did not. I listened to... other voices."

Liam's words. Megan's videos. All the proof that other riders seemed to glide through heat and pressure without blinking.

Luke watched her for a moment.

"Clara," he said. "Look at me."

She forced herself to meet his eyes.

"Growth is not a straight line," he said. "It never has been. You had a good spring, and part of you expected summer to rise in a perfect path from there. It will not. There will be stumbles and days that feel like going backwards. That does not mean you have failed."

"I nearly fell again," she whispered.

"And you did not," he replied. "You adjusted. You listened at the end, even if you did not at the start. That is still growth. Messy growth, but growth."

He stepped back and nodded toward the far end of the arena.

"Take him for a long walk on a loose rein," he said. "Let his muscles cool slowly. Then straight to the wash rack. I will bring cold water and ice if we need it."

Clara nodded, throat tight. She loosened the reins and asked Aspen to walk. He moved forward obediently but with a tired sag to his frame.

"I am so sorry," she whispered again.

He flicked one ear back as if to say it was already forgotten, that he was simply relieved to be walking instead of trotting through more grids.

At the rail, Megan watched with a faint frown.

"That looked rough," she remarked to Jenna once Clara had passed. "He stumbled over the easiest line in the ring."

Jenna gave her a look. "It is ninety degrees in here. Every horse is tired."

"Evermore is fine," Megan replied. "We did the whole grid twice without a problem."

"Good for you," Jenna said, a little sharper than usual.

Megan shrugged and reached for her water bottle.

Later that afternoon, Clara helped hose Aspen down, letting cool water run along his legs and chest. He sighed deeply, lip drooping, eyes half closed in relief. She scraped the water off and started again, careful not to shock his system with anything too cold too fast.

The heat pressed down even in the wash rack. Drops of water from the hose landed on Clara's bare arms and evaporated almost instantly. Her hair stuck to the back of her neck.

"You did not let me fall," she murmured to Aspen. "And I almost did not deserve that."

A breeze drifted through the open side of the barn, carrying with it the sound of a trailer pulling into the gravel parking area. Clara glanced toward the entrance.

A sleek dark truck, followed by a well polished trailer with a familiar crest painted on the side, rolled to a stop. The Knightfall emblem glinted in the sunlight.

Her heart sank.

"Seriously?" she muttered.

Luke appeared at her shoulder, squinting toward the driveway.

"They were supposed to arrive tomorrow," he said. "Looks like their schedule changed."

As the trailer ramp lowered, Clara glimpsed a pair of black legs and a familiar powerful neck.

Knightfall. In all his glossy, restless glory.

He snorted loudly at the heavy heat, pawed the ramp, and tossed his head in irritation.

Even from this distance, Clara could see the tension in his body. The heat did not suit him either. It pressed on his nerves, strung them tight. If he reacted like this in the stillness of the driveway, she could only imagine what he would do in a crowded warm up ring under summer sun.

A shiver ran down her spine that had nothing to do with the hose water on her shoes.

Luke followed her gaze and nodded slowly.

"There," he said. "That is what I want you to remember. The heat does not care how expensive or talented a horse is. It tests all of them. Knightfall included."

As they watched, the stallion threw his head again and slammed a hoof on the ramp in impatience. The trailer rocked.

"Warm up will be interesting with him around," Luke added thoughtfully. "For everyone."

The image of Knightfall dancing at the edge of a crowded warm up ring imprinted itself in Clara's mind. Horses dodging his sudden leaps. Riders tightening their reins. Aspen feeling that storm of agitation and trying to make sense of it.

Another piece of foreshadowing quietly slid into place, though Clara did not yet know its full shape.

She turned back to Aspen and let the cool water run in one last smooth line along his shoulder.

"We will be ready," she whispered, more to herself than to anyone else.

Ready for heat. Ready for pressure. Ready for the moments when growth did not feel like winning at all, but like stumbling and getting back up.

If she could remember that, maybe the path ahead would feel less like a straight climb and more like what it truly was, a winding trail that twisted through storms and heat and hard lessons, and still led forward, step by step.

4

The temperature broke overnight. After a week of stifling heat, a crisp breeze rolled through Willowcreek at dawn, scattering the last of the dusty haze and leaving the valley washed clean and sharp. The creek glimmered beneath fresh sunlight. Birds darted between fence posts. Even the horses moved with renewed life, their coats lifted by the cool wind.

Clara stood at the stable entrance with her helmet in hand, watching the morning unfold. Aspen grazed in the paddock, tail swishing, his energy brighter and steadier than it had been during the heatwave. She breathed out slowly, grateful for the relief.

Today was the full joint clinic with Knightfall.

Amber Leigh would be teaching. Liam would be riding. And Clara could already feel the pressure pushing against her ribs, slow and insistent.

She tried to shake it off and focused on Aspen. He lifted his head when she approached, ears pricked, eyes soft and bright. She scratched the base of his mane and smiled.

"You look ready for anything," Clara whispered. "Unlike me."

Aspen breathed into her palm, warm and reassuring.

Luke's voice carried from the barn aisle. "Clara, when you are done with Aspen, tack him in the indoor. Amber wants to start with flatwork evaluations."

Clara nodded. "Be right there."

Inside, the barn buzzed with nervous excitement. Riders tightened girths, polished boots, and talked in hushed tones about the Knightfall riders who would be joining them. Jenna adjusted her mare's bridle for the tenth time. Lara brushed imaginary dust from her saddle.

"Do you think Amber is strict?" Jenna whispered.

"Very," Lara replied. "My cousin rode in one of her clinics. She said Amber can watch you for three seconds and then tell you everything you have been doing wrong for the past six months."

Jenna blanched. "Wonderful."

Megan strutted past them, her grooming impeccable and Evermore polished to a shine. She gave Clara a pointed smile.

"Ready for your big day, Clara?" she asked.

Clara tightened Aspen's girth and forced a calm exhale. "As ready as I can be."

"You will be fine," Megan said sweetly. "Knightfall trainers love potential. They are experts at spotting weaknesses before they become habits."

Clara could not tell if it was encouragement or a warning.

She led Aspen toward the indoor arena, where two Knightfall horses were already warming up. One was the familiar black stallion, Knightfall, tossing his head with restless energy. The other was a sleek bay mare with a deep chest and elegant stride, her coat gleaming like burnished bronze. Liam rode Knightfall, posture tall and balanced, guiding the powerful stallion with subtle aids.

Amber Leigh stood near the center of the arena, speaking quietly with Luke. She wore a fitted navy jacket with the Knightfall crest, her blonde hair tied back in a neat twist. Her eyes moved constantly, tracking each horse with unwavering precision.

Clara swallowed as she entered. She dismounted to tighten Aspen's girth one last time before mounting. Her hands shook slightly, but she tried to hide it.

Amber turned toward her with a level, appraising gaze.

"Clara Bennett," Amber said. "You had a strong spring season."

Clara blinked. "You... know my name?"

Amber nodded once. "I review riders before clinics. Helps me understand what I am working with."

Clara mounted quickly, hoping Amber did not notice her boots slipping slightly against the stirrups.

"Alright riders," Amber called. "We begin with a long walk on a loose rein. I want your horses relaxed but attentive. You should already be thinking about balance, straightness, and rhythm."

Clara guided Aspen into a walk, letting the reins slip through her fingers until they rested lightly in her hands. Aspen stretched his neck forward, sniffing the air, calm for now.

Amber walked past each pair, noting posture, rein length, leg position.

When she reached Clara, she spoke without slowing.

"Relax your lower back," she said. "You ride a sensitive horse. If your body is tense, he will mirror it."

Clara exhaled and softened her hips. Amber nodded faintly.

"Better."

The warm up continued. They moved into trot, then canter work. Aspen responded willingly, his stride longer and more fluid than the previous days. Clara felt a flicker of pride. Maybe today would go well.

Amber moved to the center and raised her voice.

"Clara, bring him to me. Let me see your canter transition."

Clara nudged Aspen forward. He shifted into canter with a small surge, ears flicking back for a moment before settling.

Amber studied them with a critical eye.

"Your inside hand is too tight," she said. "Soften your fingers.

Allow his neck to stretch. He wants to move forward, but you are blocking him."

Clara complied, loosening her grip slightly. Aspen's canter smoothed out instantly.

"Good. Now engage your core. Keep your shoulders steady. Do not collapse at the inside hip."

Clara corrected the posture, feeling how deeply Amber's advice cut through layers of habit.

"Excellent. You have good feel, Clara," Amber added, her tone cool but not unkind. "But you must trust him more. Do not ride as if he will break."

The words stung more than Clara expected. She swallowed and nodded.

Amber walked away to observe Jenna next.

Luke caught Clara's eye and gave a small nod, a silent you are doing fine.

But Clara was not sure she believed it.

After warm up came the gymnastic lines. Poles and small verticals arranged in bending shapes and straight paths, each designed to test balance and responsiveness.

Clara lined up for the first exercise. Aspen's ears twitched as he studied the poles. He looked alert, ready, almost eager. Clara breathed deeply.

"Let us trust each other," she whispered.

They approached the first line. Aspen lifted cleanly, landing soft and steady. Clara kept her hands low and elastic, doing exactly as Amber had said. The rhythm felt strong, almost effortless.

Amber's voice carried across the sand.

"Better, Clara. That is how he needs you to ride."

Clara's heart swelled. Maybe this was her turning point. Maybe Amber would see how much potential Aspen held.

Then Amber added, "But his natural scope may not take him into the upper medal heights."

Clara's heart thudded.

She blinked, unsure if she heard correctly.

Amber stood with her arms crossed, watching intently.

"He has ability," Amber continued. "Good balance. Good temperament. But he is not as bold as some. At higher heights, bolder horses thrive. Sensitive ones struggle."

Clara felt her throat tighten. "He... has jumped higher before."

Amber shrugged. "He can make the height. The question is whether he can carry medal round pressure at that height."

Clara bit the inside of her cheek.

Aspen snorted beneath her, as if sensing her shift in mood.

"Ride the next line," Amber said, already turning to address another rider.

Clara guided Aspen forward again, but her confidence had cracked. The rhythm faltered. Aspen sensed the hesitation instantly and jumped with a slight twist that threw Clara off balance.

She caught herself quickly, but the mistake stung.

Was she pushing Aspen too far?

Was ambition blinding her to the truth?

Her heart hammered in her chest.

Liam entered the line behind her with Knightfall. The stallion's jump was explosive, powerful, and perfectly controlled. Liam stayed steady in the saddle, expression calm, eyes focused straight ahead. His legs absorbed the movement with practiced precision.

He rode the entire grid like it was the easiest thing in the world.

Megan clapped lightly as he landed.

"Perfect as always," she remarked.

Liam slowed Knightfall to a trot, glancing at her with a faint smile. "He likes showing off."

"Yes, well, you do not exactly make it hard for him," Megan said, flipping her hair back. "You two could win anything."

Clara trotted past them, heat creeping up her neck.

Liam noticed her lingering look.

"Your horse looks tired," he said plainly. "Is he alright?"

Clara opened her mouth, then closed it. She did not trust herself to answer without sounding defensive.

Megan leaned in. "He probably needs a lighter program. Sensitive horses get overwhelmed easily."

Clara felt something in her chest twist sharply.

Amber motioned for Liam to take the oxer. He guided Knightfall toward the higher jump, and the stallion burst forward in a perfect, powerful arc. His landing was flawless. Riders at the rail murmured in admiration.

Clara watched, admiration mixed with something heavier. Liam rode with almost unfair simplicity. No hesitation. No fear. No second guessing.

Beside that, Clara felt suddenly small.

Amber gathered the riders for final notes.

"Liam, as expected, strong work," she said. "Your eye for distance is excellent."

Liam nodded once, accepting the praise without gloating.

"Megan," Amber continued. "Good rhythm. You and Evermore communicate well."

Megan beamed.

When Amber's gaze landed on Clara, her expression softened slightly, but her tone remained factual.

"Clara. You rode with sensitivity. You made adjustments quickly. Technically, you are skilled. But you ride like someone carrying a memory of falling. Until you release that, you will not reach higher levels."

Clara swallowed. "I am working on it."

Amber nodded. "I know. And Aspen is a good horse. I do not say he cannot reach the heights. I only question whether he will enjoy that level of pressure."

Clara nodded stiffly.

Amber continued. "Some horses thrive on challenge. Some prefer steady work. And some riders must decide which path matters more, ambition or partnership."

The words sank into Clara slowly, like cold water.

Ambition or partnership.

Was she choosing one at the cost of the other?

Was she pushing Aspen because she wanted to prove herself, or because it was right for both of them?

Luke watched her quietly from the rail. He saw everything in her eyes. When the riders dispersed, he walked toward her.

"You went quiet," Luke said gently.

Clara stroked Aspen's neck, trying to steady her breathing. "She thinks Aspen might not be suited for upper medal heights."

"And what do you think?" Luke asked.

Clara hesitated. "I think she might be right. And that scares me."

Luke folded his arms, eyes soft but serious. "Amber is one perspective. A good one. But not the only one."

"She is from Knightfall," Clara whispered. "She trains champions."

"And you train your horse," Luke replied. "There is no shame in ambition. And there is no shame in choosing a different path if the one ahead does not fit."

Clara looked down at Aspen, who nudged her gently with warm breath.

"I just want to do right by him," she said.

"You will," Luke said. "Because you care enough to ask the question."

Outside, a gust of wind blew through the arena door, scattering a stack of groundlines someone had left near the corner. They rolled in strange angles, knocking into each other in a way that made Luke's eyes narrow.

"Storm must have shifted them," Jenna said from across the ring.

But Clara saw Luke's jaw tighten just slightly.

Not storm. Not wind.

Something else.

A strange prickle of unease slid along her spine, settling there like a warning.

She did not know why that small detail felt wrong.

Not yet.

But she would.

Soon.

5

The morning of the first summer medal show began with the kind of nervous energy that seeped into everything. Even the sunlight felt sharp, bouncing off trailers and silver buckles and rows of neatly oiled saddles. The show grounds buzzed with the familiar mix of excitement, competition, and just a hint of fear that always hovered beneath the surface of any big event.

Clara stepped out of the truck and shaded her eyes. The heat was not as suffocating as last week, but it pressed down with a steady insistence that made the air feel heavy. Riders bustled between stalls and grooming tents. Loudspeakers crackled to life. Somewhere near the warm up ring, a horse whinnied sharply, followed by the thud of hooves.

Aspen, tied calmly to the trailer, lifted his head at the sound. His ears twitched forward, then sideways, then forward again. Clara placed a hand on his neck, feeling the tension coil beneath the gleaming coat.

"Easy," she whispered. "We are alright. One step at a time."

Luke finished unloading the tack trunk and walked toward them, a show program tucked under his arm.

"Warm up is crowded already," he said. "Every barn seems to have arrived early. We need to be smart with our timing."

Clara nodded. She glanced toward the warm up arena and saw a sea of horses and riders weaving around each other. The tight space was alive with the sharp clip of hooves and bursts of frustrated calls from trainers.

Even from a distance, she recognized Knightfall's tall black frame. The stallion moved with an electricity that made riders instinctively shift out of his way. Liam sat tall in the saddle, cool and focused.

Clara's pulse jumped.

Before she could look away, Megan rode past on Evermore, posture perfect, smile bright. Evermore's bay coat gleamed in the sun. Megan waved at someone holding a phone.

"Just take a short clip," she said cheerfully. "High angle, okay? I want to post it before my round."

Clara rolled her eyes quietly.

Aspen snorted beside her, as if he shared the sentiment.

By the time Clara led Aspen toward the warm up arena, the tension had multiplied tenfold. Horses sidestepped and tossed their heads. Riders whispered sharp commands. Trainers stood at the edges with jump cups in hand, ready to raise or lower standards.

Aspen hesitated at the gate, as if sensing the chaos beyond.

"You can do this," Clara whispered. "I am right here."

She mounted, settled her weight, and guided him into the crowded swirl of movement. Aspen's ears flicked anxiously, body tightening under her.

A chestnut pony darted in front of them. A grey gelding swung wide on a turn. Somewhere behind her, a horse squealed in frustration.

Clara kept Aspen on a small circle away from the jumps to loosen his muscles, but every few strides he flinched at a passing horse or a loud snort.

"Deep breath," Clara murmured. "We are alright."

She repeated it again and again, as much for herself as for him.

The first real collision risk arrived early. Knightfall shot through the warm up crowd like a spark dropped into dry straw. The stallion charged into a forward canter without warning, Liam guiding him through a line of riders with bold precision.

Knightfall's sudden surge caught Aspen off guard. His head shot up. His hind legs skittered sideways. Clara reacted instantly, sitting deep, steadying her hands, bringing him back before panic could take over.

Knightfall barreled past them with inches to spare. Liam did not slow. He did not look back.

Luke did.

He strode toward the rail, voice calm but clipped.

"Liam, control your pace. This is not a private ring."

Liam glanced over his shoulder only briefly. "Knightfall needs forward momentum. He gets anxious if he feels boxed in."

Luke raised an eyebrow. "And the rest of the horses need space."

Liam lifted a shoulder in a half shrug. "Then riders should stay alert."

The message was clear. Knightfall did not adjust. Others adjusted for him.

Clara felt her jaw tighten. Aspen's breathing came faster beneath her. She stroked his neck.

"You are doing great," she whispered. "Ignore him."

Ignore Liam. Ignore Knightfall. Ignore the pressure.

But ignoring was harder than she expected.

When Clara finally guided Aspen toward the warm up jumps, she kept their expectations modest. A small vertical first. Then a slightly larger one. Aspen pricked his ears at the sight of the jump and lifted with natural ease. His landing felt smooth. His trot afterward was steady.

Clara allowed herself a tiny smile.

Then Megan swooped in on Evermore with a canter that felt more like showing off than warming up. The bay gelding launched over the oxer, clearing it by a mile. Megan's hair floated behind her in the morning breeze. She landed and guided Evermore immediately into another tight turn.

The phone-wielding friend along the rail clapped. "Perfect, Meg. Got it. You already look like a winner."

Megan turned Evermore toward the oxer again. As she passed Clara, she leaned slightly in the saddle.

"Better make your first round good," she murmured under her breath. "Judges love a good opening impression."

Clara's stomach tightened.

Aspen shook his head nervously as Evermore swept past.

Clara refocused and asked for one more warm up jump. Aspen lifted willingly again, though she could feel the tension humming in his back like a drawn string.

Luke stepped up beside the fence.

"You are ready," he said quietly. "Do not overdo the warm up. He needs freshness for the actual round."

Clara nodded. She walked Aspen toward the in-gate for her first round.

The ring looked enormous. Bright white rails gleamed under the sun. The jumps were decorated with flowers and banners. A few spectators leaned along the fence. Nothing too dramatic, and yet her chest tightened as if she were about to walk into a stadium filled with thousands.

A steward lifted a clipboard.

"Clara Bennett and Aspen. You are on deck."

Clara breathed deeply, eyes on the course.

"You know it," she whispered. "One jump at a time."

Aspen flicked an ear.

Her number was called.

She entered.

The start felt surprisingly steady.

Aspen moved into his opening canter with determination. Clara softened her reins. She focused on rhythm, not speed, just as Luke had taught her.

First jump. A small vertical with red bricks. Aspen cleared it neatly.

Second jump. A bending line. Clara kept her hands low, her body light.

Aspen stayed with her, stretching forward with a calm, consistent stride.

Halfway through the course, Clara felt a flutter of relief.

Then Liam's voice carried faintly from the rail.

"Her rhythm is good, but she keeps checking too much."

The words were not meant for her, but they sliced into her focus like a sharp edge.

Clara's shoulders stiffened.

Aspen felt it.

Their next distance came up slightly long. Aspen corrected, but the jump lost its earlier smoothness.

Clara inhaled sharply and corrected her posture.

"Stay with me," she whispered.

They reached the final line. Aspen cleared the vertical cleanly. The last oxer rose ahead, bright blue poles.

Aspen lifted. Clara followed.

They landed together, safe and steady.

A clean round.

Not bold. Not flashy. But clean.

Applause from a few spectators drifted through the air.

Clara exhaled, shaky but relieved. She patted Aspen's neck.

"You did it," she whispered.

. . .

Back at the rail, Luke smiled softly.

"Good job," he said. "Honest riding. Honest result."

Clara nodded, heart still racing. "It felt safe. Maybe too safe."

"Safe is the foundation," Luke replied.

Before he could say more, the loudspeaker boomed.

"Next to ride: Liam Carter and Knightfall."

Clara turned instinctively.

Liam guided Knightfall into the ring with a presence that shifted the air. The stallion's hooves struck the ground like drums. His neck arched. His stride carried the confidence of a horse who knew everyone was watching.

Clara held her breath as Liam began the course.

Where Clara's round had been careful, Liam's was explosive.

Knightfall attacked each jump with speed and power. He soared over the oxer with room to spare. His landing thundered across the ring.

Riders around the warm up murmured in admiration.

Luke watched with a neutral expression. "Bold," he said. "Sometimes too bold."

Clara could not look away.

Knightfall finished the course in a time that made a few riders whistle quietly.

Liam circled once, then gave a small nod toward Amber on the rail. Megan clapped enthusiastically, leaning over Evermore's neck.

"That was incredible," she called. "You two are unstoppable."

Liam smiled faintly. "He likes a challenge."

Megan trotted closer. "Maybe we should school together sometime. Evermore loves horses with that kind of energy."

Liam nodded, entertained. "We could."

Clara turned away, suddenly smaller, quieter.

Jenna nudged her gently. "Your round was good, Clara."

Clara nodded, but her chest had tightened again.

Good was not enough in this ring.

At least, that was what the pressure whispered.

She was still replaying Liam's ride in her head when Megan finished her own round. Megan had always been a strong rider, but today she added extra flair. Evermore flicked his tail dramatically over each jump. Megan sat tall, smiling at the rail between elements.

The moment her round ended, she was already pulling out her phone.

"That felt so good," she announced loudly. "I am posting the clip. Evermore is on fire today."

Clara lowered her eyes.

Aspen grazed quietly beside her, as if unaware of any spotlight he might need to chase.

Luke stepped up beside her and leaned on the fence.

"You are withdrawing again," he said softly.

Clara tried to deny it. "I am not."

He gave her a look that said he saw more than she spoke.

"You rode a clean round," Luke said. "A good round. Do not let someone else's style make you doubt your own."

Clara swallowed. "I know. It is just... Liam. And Megan. And the energy. I feel like I am always behind."

Luke shook his head. "You are not behind. You are different."

He let the words settle before continuing.

"And sometimes different is exactly what wins later, when the pressure breaks the flashy horses."

Clara stared at Aspen. His soft eyes. His steady breath. His gentle presence.

Different.

Not medal material.

Or maybe medal material in a different way.

Before she could respond, the steward called the next class.

Clara exhaled slowly.

The day was far from over, and the weight of summer had only just begun to settle on her shoulders.

And somewhere, in the back of her mind, the tension of the warm up ring, the chaos, the careless near collision with Knightfall, all planted a quiet seed.

A warning for what crowded warm ups and high stakes could do later.

Especially when sabotage touched a jump.

But that moment had not come yet.

For now, Clara stood in the heat, brushed her hand along Aspen's neck, and whispered:

"We will learn. We always do."

6

The sunlight had shifted to late afternoon gold by the time Clara brought Aspen back to the trailer. His sweat marks had dried to faint salt patches, and he lowered his head gratefully as she loosened the girth. The showgrounds hummed with the energy of riders packing up, congratulating each other, arguing quietly with trainers, or replaying their rounds through excited gestures.

Clara should have felt proud. Their first summer medal round had been clean, safe, and steady. Aspen had given her his heart in the ring. But the moment she stepped out of the arena, she had known something was coming. Something unseen but sharp.

She felt it now as she ran a damp sponge along Aspen's neck.

A buzzing shift in the air.

A whisper forming behind her.

"Clara."

Jenna approached with a tight expression, her phone held awkwardly at her side.

"You should see this before Megan shows you," Jenna said quietly. "Or before someone else does."

Clara frowned. "See what?"

Jenna hesitated, then tapped open a video.

Clara's breath caught.

On the screen were two clips placed side by side. On the left was Liam's round, bold and brilliant, Knightfall stretching over each jump as if the course belonged to him. On the right was Clara and Aspen, clean but cautious.

Above the clips was a caption in bright text.

Who has the medal season edge?

Liam Carter vs Clara Bennett

Thousands of views already. Hundreds of comments.

Clara felt a cold rush through her.

Jenna bit her lip. "I think Megan sent the video to a horse influencer page. They posted it an hour ago."

Clara scrolled through the comments.

Liam all the way.

Clara looks scared.

The chestnut horse is cute but slow.

Knightfall is a monster. Literal perfection.

Aspen is sweet but nervous.

Clara lost her edge.

Clara's stomach twisted violently.

She had known comparison would happen. She had known Liam would draw attention. But seeing their names placed together as if she were a warm up act next to a champion felt like being punched in the chest.

"Do not look at the comments," Jenna urged softly.

Clara forced herself to lock the phone and hand it back.

"Thanks," she whispered. "I need a minute."

She walked toward the barn aisle, feeling as if the ground shifted beneath her feet. The chatter around her faded into a distant hum. She passed riders brushing horses, laughing with friends, replaying their own rounds. No one paid attention to her.

The tack room door creaked as she slipped inside.

The air was cooler, dimmer, and heavy with the scent of leather and saddle soap. Bridles hung in neat rows. Saddle pads stacked in tall piles. The quiet made her chest ache.

Clara pressed her back against the wall and slid down until she was sitting on the floor, arms wrapped around her knees.

She held the silence as long as she could.

Then the tears came.

Slow at first. Then harder. The kind that made breathing feel sharp and uneven.

She remembered Amber's words. Sensitive horse. Limited scope. Pressure might break him.

She remembered Liam's voice. Sweet but not medal material.

She remembered Megan's whispers from the warm up ring. Make a good first impression.

Clara buried her face in her arms.

Nothing she did today had erased those voices.

Not even the clean round.

She felt the weight of every doubt pressing on her chest, squeezing until the tears blurred her vision.

A soft knock sounded against the doorframe.

"Clara?"

She startled, brushing her sleeve quickly across her eyes.

It was Luke.

He stepped inside without speaking and closed the door gently behind him. He lowered himself to the floor beside her, knees bent, arms resting loosely over them.

He did not touch her. He did not rush her. He simply sat there until her breathing eased.

Finally he spoke.

"Jenna told me."

Clara pressed her palms together tightly. "I am sorry. I know it was not professional to run in here and hide."

"You are allowed to have a moment," Luke said softly. "You are human."

Clara swallowed hard. "I thought I was ready for medal season. I thought after spring I could handle pressure. But the moment Liam shows up, everything I worked for feels small. Like I am pretending to compete with someone on a different level."

Luke turned his head slightly. "Is that what the comments said?"

Clara closed her eyes. "They said I lost my edge."

"And do you believe them?" Luke asked.

The question cut sharper than the comments.

Clara stared at her hands.

"I do not know," she whispered. "Maybe they are right. I felt safe today. Too safe. And Liam looked like he belonged in that ring. He made me look... slow."

Luke inhaled deeply.

"Clara," he said. "This is the part of the season they never show you in videos. The doubts. The comparisons. The temptation to measure your worth against someone else's talent."

Clara blinked tears away. "But what if Amber is right? What if Aspen is not meant for upper heights? What if I am pushing him? What if..."

She struggled to finish.

"What if I am the one who is not medal material?"

Luke turned fully toward her.

"Do you want the truth?" he asked gently.

She nodded, bracing herself.

"You could keep up with Liam," Luke said. "Not today. Not tomorrow. But in time, yes. You have the feel and the heart. And Aspen has the ability if you build him up slowly and with care."

Clara stared at him, breath held.

"But," Luke continued, "not if you train for the judges, or for the comments online, or for what Megan posts on her page."

He touched the floor lightly with one hand.

"You only move forward if you ride for yourself and your horse. Nothing else."

Clara leaned her head back against the wall, tears threatening again.

"I feel like withdrawing," she whispered. "I do not want to. But a part of me does."

Luke nodded slowly. "That is normal."

"You think so?"

"I know so," Luke said. "Any rider who has ever chased something big has had this moment. The moment when pressure outweighs joy. The moment when stepping back feels safer than stepping forward."

He paused, letting his words settle.

"What matters," he said quietly, "is that you decide from a place of truth. Not fear."

Clara closed her eyes tightly.

Her truth felt tangled in a knot she could not untie. She wanted to ride. She wanted to improve. She wanted to believe Aspen could rise with her. But she also feared losing him to pressure, or losing herself to comparison.

Luke stood slowly and offered her his hand.

"Come on," he said. "Let us help Aspen."

Back at the trailer, Aspen lifted his head the moment Clara approached. His ears flicked forward, searching for her expression.

He sensed everything.

Clara stroked his muzzle. "I am sorry," she whispered. "I let other people's voices get into my head."

Aspen's nostrils flared softly, and he leaned into her palm.

Luke watched them with quiet understanding.

"His stride is short today," Luke said. "He senses your tension. Horses like Aspen mirror emotion before they mirror technique."

Clara nodded, feeling guilt twist in her stomach. "I know."

"You need a different training plan," Luke said. "One designed to build confidence, not flash."

Clara looked up. "Confidence?"

"For both of you," Luke said. "You are not competing with Liam. You are competing with who you were last month. That is your only opponent."

Clara felt her chest loosen slightly.

Her only opponent was herself.

Luke cleared his throat softly. "We will lighten the schedule. More quiet hacks. More rhythm work. Shorter sessions. Less pressure. Medal season is not a sprint. It is a series of moments stacked together. You do not have to win the season in one weekend."

Clara watched Aspen drop his head to graze beside the trailer.

"I do not want to withdraw," she whispered. "Not deep down. But I do not want to break him either."

"You will not," Luke said firmly. "Because you are asking the right questions."

Clara breathed out slowly.

The comments still hurt. Megan's whispers still stung. Liam's precision still intimidated her. But a tiny spark inside her, one that had dimmed earlier, flickered back to life.

"We will try again," she said.

Aspen lifted his head as if he had been waiting for her to say it.

Luke smiled. "Good."

As Clara unbuckled Aspen's bridle, she thought of the long road ahead. The shows. The pressure. The warm up chaos. The comparisons. The unknown challenges.

She did not know it yet, but the storm inside her had only begun to build.

And in Chapter 9, that storm would break open.

But for now, she focused on one thing.

Her hand on Aspen's steady neck, her breath slowing to match his, and the quiet truth that whispered beneath the fear.

She was not done yet.

Not even close.

7

The morning after the medal show should have felt quieter. Softer. A chance for Clara to reset and breathe again. But as soon as she stepped out of the truck at Willowcreek, the air felt charged with something restless. Not the calm-before-a-storm kind of charge. Something sharper. Something that hinted at friction beneath the surface.

A line of horse trailers stood parked along the gravel drive. More than usual. A few she did not recognise. And the low rumble of voices echoed from the indoor arena long before Clara reached the barn.

She frowned.

"Luke said today was a light schooling day," Clara said to Aspen, who walked beside her with his nose nudging the end of the lead rope. "So who is here this early?"

Aspen flicked an ear but said nothing, of course. His stride felt slow, steady, and healing from yesterday's tension. Clara had made their ride deliberately short and gentle that morning, guiding him through the grassy path along the creek. He had seemed grateful, dropping his head and blinking in that soft, thoughtful way of his.

Now, as they approached the barn, the energy around them shifted.

Knightfall's truck was parked near the arena entrance.

Clara felt her stomach tighten.

"They did not say anything about coming today," she whispered.

Aspen halted mid step, ears pricked sharply.

Clara stepped closer to reassure him, smoothing a hand along his warm neck.

Inside the barn aisle, riders clustered in little pockets. Jenna, Lara, and a few others stood near the bulletin board, talking in low voices that carried tension, not excitement.

When they saw Clara, Jenna hurried toward her.

"You heard?" Jenna asked.

"Heard what?" Clara replied.

"Knightfall is here," Lara whispered. "Not Amber this time. Some of their riders. Including Liam."

Clara's pulse stumbled.

"What? Why?"

"No idea," Jenna said. "They showed up early and started warming up in the indoor without talking to Luke. Apparently they said their arena is being redone and they needed a space to ride."

Clara clenched her jaw. "They could have asked."

"They did ask," Lara said. "Just not first. They asked while they were already unloading."

Clara looked toward the open arena door. She could hear the rhythmic pounding of hooves on sand. The sharp intake and release of horse breaths. The clipped commands of someone giving strong cues.

Knightfall.

Aspen tensed beside her, lifting his head high. His eyes widened.

"It is alright," Clara whispered. "We are just walking."

But her voice trembled slightly.

She led Aspen to his stall to tack him up, trying to stay focused. She brushed his coat until the copper shine returned. She checked his hooves, running a finger along the frog to remove packed dirt. He shifted, uneasy. His ears remained pinned toward the indoor.

The sound of a powerful, dramatic snort echoed through the arena.

Knightfall's voice.

Aspen stiffened.

Clara stroked his shoulder. "I know. I know. We will go slow."

She hoped those words comforted him. She hoped they comforted her too.

In the indoor arena, heat and tension mixed like something volatile. Sunlight filtered in long golden slants through the open side doors, lighting up dust floating through the air. But all Clara could focus on was the black horse at the center of it all.

Knightfall cannoned around the arena in a broad canter, Liam sitting tall and balanced despite the stallion's extra energy. Knight-fall snorted repeatedly, pawing at the air between strides as though annoyed at the sun, the dust, the walls, and the mere existence of other horses.

Luke stood on the far side of the arena with a tight expression, arms crossed.

Megan was perched on Evermore near the rail, as if waiting for a spotlight to turn toward her. Meanwhile, two Knightfall riders schooled their horses at the opposite end. The tension of too many egos and too many strong horses in too small a space felt like a storm about to break.

Clara hesitated at the doorway.

Should she even bring Aspen in?

He lowered his head briefly, then lifted it sharply as Knightfall executed a flying change that looked more like showing off than training. The stallion flung his front legs forward in an extravagant display before collecting again.

Aspen's muscles bunched beneath his skin. Clara felt the tremor travel through the lead rope.

She swallowed.

"We will take it slow," she whispered.

She breathed deeply, mounted, and walked Aspen into the arena.

The moment they entered, she felt him shrink beneath her. His walk went tight, short, almost mincing. His ears pinned backward toward Knightfall's relentless energy.

"It is alright," Clara murmured. "Ignore him. Focus on us."

Aspen flicked his tail anxiously.

Liam noticed them and eased Knightfall into a slower trot, as if observing how Aspen would react. His gaze landed on Clara for half a second before his attention returned to Knightfall's explosive movement.

Clara bit her lip and guided Aspen along the outer rail. They walked for several laps, letting the warm up stretch his muscles. Aspen's stride lengthened slightly as he relaxed under Clara's seat. She breathed in and matched her rhythm to his.

Then everything changed in a single heartbeat.

Knightfall surged into a forward canter so quickly that Clara barely processed it. He thundered across the arena diagonally, cutting straight through the path of another rider. The girl squeaked, yanking her mare aside.

Aspen jolted.

Clara steadied him immediately, her seat deep, her hands soft.

"Easy," she whispered.

But Knightfall did not slow. Liam leaned into the movement, almost enjoying the display of raw power.

Luke stepped toward the rail.

"Liam," he called. His tone was even, but Clara could hear the warning beneath it. "Control your pace."

Liam nodded, but the apology was thin. Knightfall danced sideways, chest lifted, hooves striking the sand with an impatient beat.

Clara forced Aspen back onto a circle. She kept her focus on her own horse, but her hands trembled slightly.

Megan saw it.

Her voice drifted across the arena, honeyed and sharp.

"Is Aspen alright?" Megan asked. "He looks so jumpy today."

Clara forced her jaw to unclench. "He is fine. It is just crowded."

Megan shrugged delicately. "Maybe the pressure is too much for him. Sensitive horses get overwhelmed."

Clara's grip tightened on the reins.

Jenna shot her a sympathetic look from across the arena.

Clara ignored the sting and prepared to move Aspen into a trot. But before she could give the cue, Liam guided Knightfall into a collected canter right behind her.

The stallion pranced dangerously close.

Clara stiffened. Aspen's ears flew backward. His tail flicked in agitation.

Liam called out, "Passing on the inside."

There was no space for that.

Clara opened her mouth to protest just as Liam urged Knightfall through the gap.

Aspen panicked. His back rounded. His stride shortened. His hindquarters shifted sideways.

Clara reacted fast, instinctively lifting her hands and steadying her seat. Aspen hopped forward, almost losing his balance.

Luke shouted across the arena.

"Liam. Enough."

This time the warning was not subtle.

Liam slowed Knightfall immediately but did not apologise. He simply touched the stallion's neck and said quietly, "He needs this practice too."

Clara stared at him, stunned.

Practice?

Panic flared in her chest. Her confidence, already brittle, cracked.

She guided Aspen toward the far end of the arena, away from Knightfall's reach.

Her breathing was too fast.

Her hands trembled again.

Aspen sensed it and responded with more worry.

Luke approached her at the fence, expression controlled but tight.

"Clara," he said quietly. "Walk him. Breathe. You are feeding him your stress."

"I know," Clara whispered. "But that was too close. He nearly—"

"You are alright," Luke said. "He is alright. Stay in your bubble. Ignore Knightfall."

Clara tried. She truly tried.

But her chest felt tight, her thoughts loud, her nerves raw.

She circled Aspen until his stride settled, but the tension in her heart remained. She wanted to be brave. She wanted to rise. But Liam's presence made her feel small again, and Aspen's fear made her feel guilty for dragging him into this world.

Megan trotted past, smiling at Liam. "Knightfall looks incredible today. He is so sharp. You two make everyone else look like warm up riders."

Liam shrugged. "We train hard."

Megan tossed her hair. "Some horses were born for competitive rings."

Her eyes flicked deliberately toward Clara.

Clara felt the cut.

Aspen stumbled slightly beneath her seat.

She steadied him.

But something inside her began to retreat.

Quietly.

Deeply.

Luke saw it immediately.

He walked toward her again, slower this time, expression softening.

"Clara," he said quietly. "Talk to me."

Clara shook her head. "Not now."

"Then breathe," Luke said. "You are going somewhere in your mind. Come back."

Clara swallowed thickly. "I... I am fine."

"You are not," Luke said gently.

Aspen snorted, shifting nervously.

Luke rested a hand lightly on Aspen's neck, grounding them both.

"This is too much stimulation," he said. "Not just for you. For him too. You know he feeds off the energy around him. Knightfall is a storm in a bottle. Any horse would be unsettled."

Clara closed her eyes.

"I thought I was getting stronger," she whispered.

"You are," Luke said. "But strength does not protect you from being overwhelmed. It helps you recover afterward."

Clara's shoulders shook. Not crying. Just near breaking.

Luke lowered his voice. "You are not losing. You are learning."

Clara blinked at him, eyes burning.

He stepped back. "Take a break. Walk him outside. Fresh air will help."

Clara nodded, throat tight.

She guided Aspen to the gate, heart heavy, breath brittle. Aspen exhaled in relief the moment they stepped outside into open space.

The sun warmed her back. The breeze brushed her cheek.

She inhaled slowly.

Aspen lowered his head, breathing deeply.

"I am sorry," Clara whispered. "I am trying."

But a whisper found its way through her thoughts.

Maybe Megan was right.

Maybe Aspen was too sensitive.

Maybe she was too.

Maybe they were not built for medal ring pressure.

The doubts curled around her heart like smoke.

And little did she know, someone else at Willowcreek that day was watching the pressure build. Watching the way poles were left near the jump storage. Watching the way certain riders paid attention to height adjustments.

A detail that would matter very soon.

But not yet.

For now, Clara stood in the sunlight with Aspen grazing quietly beside her, unaware that trouble at Willowcreek had only just begun.

———

Clara walked Aspen slowly along the outer track behind the indoor arena, letting the sun and breeze settle her rattled nerves. Aspen's head dropped naturally as he munched at stray grass tufts peeking through the packed dirt. His tail swished with a steady rhythm, no longer sharp and anxious.

Clara's heart settled too, but not as quickly or as easily. Her chest still felt tight, and every deep breath caught slightly at the top.

She wanted to be strong. She wanted to shake off Liam's careless riding, Megan's competitive smirk, and the pressure that clung to every inch of the warm up arena.

But she could not lie to herself.

She had been shaken.

And worse, Aspen had been shaken too.

She leaned against the fence while Aspen grazed, her fingers tangled loosely in his mane.

"I wish he would not get so close," she whispered softly. "Knightfall scares you. And honestly he scares me too."

Aspen lifted his head for a moment as if listening. Then he nudged Clara's shoulder gently, his warm breath soft on her skin.

She smiled faintly. "I know. You are trying."

Her voice cracked slightly.

"I am trying too."

The path around the back of the arena was peaceful now, but

sounds drifted from the indoor, faint but pointed. Hooves pounding. Megan's laugh. The sharp instructions of one of the Knightfall riders.

Clara tried to ignore it.

But part of her felt left out again. On the outside of a world that seemed to orbit Liam.

He rode like someone who belonged in that pressure. Someone who thrived in chaos.

Clara rode like someone who held her breath, even when she tried not to.

After a few long minutes, she felt her breathing steady enough to return.

"Ready?" she whispered, gently tugging the lead rope.

Aspen lifted his head and followed, though his ears flicked toward the indoor again. Clara rubbed his neck.

"We will not stay long," she promised.

When they reentered the arena, it was marginally calmer. One of the Knightfall riders was packing up. Megan and Evermore were cantering slowly, both looking polished and pleased.

Liam had dismounted Knightfall and stood near the rail speaking with Amber, who had arrived just moments earlier. Amber listened with her arms crossed, her expression thoughtful. Knightfall stood beside Liam, blowing softly, his muscles rippling with each shift of weight.

Clara felt Aspen tense beneath her again, but not as sharply as earlier.

Luke waved her over.

"We will do some quiet trot work on the outer track," he said. "Nothing fancy. I want you to leave this session feeling successful."

Clara nodded, grateful beyond words.

She gathered the reins and nudged Aspen into a trot. His stride was steady, slightly shorter than usual but no longer braced. Clara focused on breathing out slowly each time her seat settled.

One-two. One-two. One-two.

It soothed her.

Luke watched for a full lap and then nodded.

"There you go," he said. "Better. Now follow the quarter line. Keep him straight. Let the rhythm guide you."

Clara tried.

Aspen's trot evened further. His neck loosened. His ears flicked back and forth, listening to her instead of Knightfall. For a few precious minutes, the world shrank to just them.

She almost felt like herself again.

Almost.

Until Megan's voice drifted through the air.

"I still cannot believe Liam fit Knightfall through that tight gap earlier. That stallion is practically a machine. If I tried that with Evermore, we would both be on the ground."

Liam merely lifted an eyebrow. "Knightfall handles pressure."

Clara's grip tightened unconsciously, and Aspen felt it at once. His head popped up. His stride shortened.

Luke noticed immediately.

"Clara," he said softly. "Stay with him. Do not let someone else take you out of your body."

Clara blinked, realising how quickly the old tension tried to reclaim her.

"You are right," she said. "Sorry."

"You do not have to apologise for being human," Luke replied.

She breathed out slowly. "I just want to be better."

"You will be," Luke said. "But not by comparing yourself to someone who rides a completely different kind of horse."

Clara nodded, though some part of her did not believe herself yet.

After another lap, Luke motioned her toward the center of the arena.

"That is enough for today," he said kindly. "You did what you needed to do. End on a good note."

Clara exhaled a long breath of relief.

"Thank you," she whispered. "Really. Thank you."

Luke gave a small smile. "Go cool him out outside. Then take the rest of the day off from training. Your brain needs quiet just as much as your horse does."

Clara nodded gratefully and guided Aspen toward the gate.

But before she reached it, Megan intercepted her.

"Leaving already?" Megan asked, tone deceptively sweet.

"We had a good session," Clara said simply.

"Good," Megan replied. "You will need it."

Clara frowned. "Need what?"

"For the next show," Megan said with a tilt of her head. "Liam is riding the same classes as you. And Knightfall is... intense. If you thought today was chaotic, wait until you see warm up at a medal qualifier."

Clara's stomach tightened.

Megan continued with a bright smile. "Better keep Aspen focused. Sensitive horses get overwhelmed."

Clara swallowed. "He is trying his best."

Megan's smile softened. "I know. And you are too."

Somehow, that did not feel comforting.

Clara walked away before her voice betrayed her.

Aspen nuzzled her shoulder when they stepped into the sunlight again, as if sensing her distress.

Her throat tightened.

Back at the barn, Clara let Aspen graze again near the paddocks. The rhythmic sound of his chewing soothed her. Birds sang from the hedges. A distant tractor rumbled along the ridge on the far side of the property.

Clara leaned against the fence and stared at the grass.

Her mind spun in slow circles.

She wanted to keep going.

She wanted to get stronger.

She wanted to prove she could handle medals.

She wanted to ride with confidence and joy.

But she also wanted to run away from the pressure.

To hide from judgment.

To protect Aspen from environments that shook him to his core.

And to protect herself from feelings that left her breathless.

The conflict twisted inside her like two vines pulling in opposite directions.

"Clara."

She turned.

Luke approached with a thoughtful expression.

He stopped beside her, one hand resting lightly on the fence.

"I saw your face when Megan spoke to you."

Clara attempted a weak smile. "I thought I hid it."

"You never hide anything from your horse," Luke said simply. "I see it through him."

Clara's shoulders sagged.

Luke studied her gently. "Talk to me."

Clara hesitated, then spoke truthfully.

"I do not know if I can do medal season," she said softly. "Every time Liam rides, I feel small. Every time Knightfall enters a ring, Aspen panics. And every time Megan speaks, I second guess everything I thought I had gained back."

She looked down at her hands.

"Maybe Amber is right," she whispered. "Maybe Aspen is not made for this level. Maybe I am not."

Luke let her words settle in the warm air between them.

When he finally spoke, his voice was calm.

"The decision is yours," he said. "But you are not at the end of anything. You are in the middle of learning. The messy middle.

Where doubts feel bigger than reward and pressure feels heavier than progress."

Clara blinked back sudden tears.

Luke continued. "You have not failed. You have not fallen behind. You are in a growth period, and they are almost always uncomfortable."

Clara breathed shakily. "It feels like everyone else is moving forward and I am stuck."

"That is because you are looking at their highlights," Luke said. "Not their struggles. Liam fights Knightfall every day. Megan fights her own image more than you know."

Clara stared at him. "How do you stay so calm?"

Luke smiled faintly. "Practice."

He nudged Aspen's shoulder gently. "Ride your journey, Clara. Not theirs."

Clara wiped her eyes with the back of her hand.

"I want to," she whispered. "I really do."

"And you will," Luke said. "You just need one moment to tip the balance in the right direction. It has not arrived yet. But it is coming."

Clara looked up at him.

"When?" she whispered.

Luke tapped her lightly on the shoulder.

"Chapter nine," he said with a half smile.

Clara laughed through her tears despite herself.

The knot inside her loosened. Not undone. But looser.

Aspen lifted his head to nuzzle her again.

She rested her forehead against his.

"We will keep going," she whispered. "Slowly. Carefully. But we will keep going."

Luke stepped back, satisfied.

"Good," he said simply. "Go home. Rest. Tomorrow we start fresh."

Clara nodded.

She led Aspen toward his paddock, sunlight casting long

shadows across the grass. She unclipped his lead rope and watched him trot forward, tail lifted, energy returning.

He paused halfway across the field and turned toward her.

As if asking.

Are you still with me?

Clara's heart softened.

"Yes," she whispered. "Always."

But neither of them knew that trouble was still unraveling slowly in the background.

Small things.

Out-of-place poles.

Shuffled groundlines.

Someone observing how adjustments changed distances.

Quiet signs.

Harmless now.

Not harmless later.

For now, Clara walked back toward the barn, unaware that her quiet steps were leading her toward the storm that would change everything.

8

The second summer medal qualifier began with an uneasy quiet. Not the peaceful kind. The kind that settled into Clara's bones and refused to move. She felt it the moment she stepped out of the truck. The sky was too clear. The breeze too still. Even the showground seemed to hold its breath.

Aspen walked beside her, ears flicking steadily, alert to every sound. He had recovered well from the previous week, but he still carried the memory of Knightfall's chaos in the warm up ring. His stride was careful today, and Clara knew exactly why.

They both sensed something.

Luke unloaded the tack trunk and glanced around, jaw set in a thoughtful line.

"Show looks crowded," he said. "More barns than last time."

Clara followed his gaze. Riding school ponies. Warmblood jumpers. Hunters from two towns over. And near the competition arena, a cluster of riders in matching navy jackets with the Knightfall crest.

Clara's stomach tightened.

Liam was among them, adjusting Knightfall's bridle with practiced ease. The black stallion's ears flicked in every direction, restless and dangerous. Even from a distance, Clara could feel the storm inside him.

Megan spotted Clara and waved from atop Evermore, who dazzled in the sunlight, every braid perfect, every step precise.

"Good luck today," Megan called sweetly. "The lines look technical. I hope Aspen is ready."

Clara forced a smile she did not feel. "Thanks. You too."

Megan's smile grew. "I always am."

Aspen shifted beside Clara as if reacting to the energy around Evermore and Knightfall.

"It is alright," Clara whispered, stroking Aspen's neck. "We have practiced. We can do this."

But the worry sat stubbornly in her chest.

Warm up was worse than before.

Riders swerved around each other. Jumps were being raised, lowered, then raised again without warning. Trainers barked orders. Hooves churned the sand in frantic patterns. Dust lifted with each landing.

Knightfall weaved through the chaos like a live wire, his neck arched, his breath loud. Liam rode him with determination and focus, but even he had to fight for control. Twice Knightfall threatened to rear. Once he struck out with a front hoof when another horse moved too close.

Aspen flinched every time.

Clara walked him along the outside rail, trying to ease him into the rhythm of the arena. She kept her hands soft, her breath even. Aspen softened for a moment, only to stiffen again when Knightfall powered past.

Clara held her composure, but each pass rattled her.

Jenna rode by on her paint gelding, cheeks flushed with heat and nerves.

"You alright?" she whispered.

Clara nodded, though the truth felt heavier. "Trying to be."

Jenna offered a small, sympathetic smile. "Stay focused on your bubble. Luke always says that."

Clara returned the smile, grateful. She had no idea how much she needed that reminder.

The warm up jumps looked high today. Higher than they should have before the first round. A few riders hesitated before approaching.

Clara guided Aspen toward the smallest vertical. He perked his ears forward, preparing to jump.

Then Knightfall exploded into the line beside them, his front hooves lifting, hindquarters springing forward. His tail whipped. His nostrils flared.

Aspen startled sideways so sharply that Clara's stirrup nearly slipped from her foot.

"Whoa," Clara breathed, steadying him with both hands.

Liam slowed Knightfall and offered a brief, detached apology. "Sorry. He is wound up. We need forward momentum."

Clara forced a breath and nodded.

Aspen trembled beneath her for several seconds. His eyes were wide. His breathing fast.

Luke appeared at Clara's knee, calm but alert.

"You alright?" he asked.

"Yes," Clara said quietly. "He is just nervous."

"He is handling more than most horses would," Luke said firmly. "Give him credit. And give yourself some too."

Clara nodded.

They tried again.

Aspen approached the small vertical. He lifted cleanly, landing balanced, though his stride afterward was tight, shorter than usual.

Clara softened her reins. "Good boy," she murmured.

Luke waved her over.

"That is enough for warm up," he said. "Do not overdo it. Take him out. Walk him. Keep his brain quiet."

Clara nodded and guided Aspen out of the chaos. As soon as they stepped into open space, Aspen lowered his head with an exhale.

Clara stroked his neck, relieved.

But inside, her nerves stretched thin.

Her round was second in the class.

She could feel her pulse in her throat as she approached the in gate. Aspen walked beside her with alert eyes, ears flicking rapidly. The announcer called the first rider's time and score.

Then the loudspeaker crackled.

"Next to ride, Clara Bennett on Aspen from Willowcreek Stables."

Clara mounted, tightened the girth one last time, and guided Aspen into the ring.

The world narrowed.

The bright poles.

The banners fluttering.

The faint hum of spectators.

The curve of each jump line.

The pressure.

She breathed once, deeply.

Then she asked Aspen to canter.

He stepped into it willingly, though a slight hesitation lingered in his stride.

Clara sat tall and found their rhythm. One-two-one-two. Aspen's strides matched her seat. They approached the first vertical.

Aspen lifted cleanly.

Clara exhaled in relief.

Second jump. A line that required careful distance. Aspen cleared it.

Third jump. A sharp turn into a vertical. Aspen hesitated for half a second, but Clara guided him gently and he jumped softly.

Clara smiled for the first time that day.

"We have this," she whispered.

But as they approached the fourth jump, something shifted.

A small oxer with a white groundline. Except the groundline looked slightly... off.

Clara blinked, confused.

It was set too far back. Not enough to be obvious to a spectator. But enough to change Aspen's perception of the takeoff point.

He slowed.

Clara steadied him. "It is alright. You can do this."

But Aspen's stride shortened sharply. His ears flicked back, then forward, then back again. He lifted his front feet at an awkward moment, panic spreading like a ripple through his muscles.

Clara felt it instantly.

Something was wrong with the jump.

Something small.

Something dangerous.

She reached her decision in a heartbeat.

She pulled Aspen out of the line.

The crowd murmured.

Clara circled him once, her breath shaking.

The course steward ran toward her. "Are you withdrawing?"

"No," Clara said quickly. "The groundline is off."

The steward blinked, confused, then looked at the jump. His eyes widened. He waved a flag to halt the round.

Luke leapt from the rail and reached the jump within seconds. He crouched, measured with his eye, and his jaw tightened.

Someone had moved the groundline back. Far enough to be dangerous.

Clara's gut twisted.

She felt the pressure in her chest rising.

The fear Aspen felt.

The instinct she had trusted.

Luke fixed the groundline with swift, precise movements. Then he stood, brushing sand from his hands.

"Good call," he said to Clara. "You kept him safe."

Her eyes burned. "Someone moved it."

Luke's jaw tightened. "I know."

The steward gave her permission to restart.

Clara swallowed hard and guided Aspen back into their canter.

His stride was trembling now. His trust shaken. He lifted over the newly fixed jump, but his landing was tight and uneven.

Clara steadied him. "Almost done. You are doing so well."

They finished the last two jumps slowly, carefully. No faults. But the rhythm was gone. The confidence was cracked.

Clara exited the arena with a tight throat.

Her score was posted as clear with time faults.

Not last.

Not terrible.

Not the ride she wanted.

Aspen breathed heavily. Clara stroked his neck, guilt curling in her stomach.

"You were brave," she whispered. "Braver than me."

Megan trotted up on Evermore, phone in hand.

"Clara, I heard what happened," she said. "Someone said you pulled out because Aspen got scared."

Clara blinked. "The groundline was wrong."

Megan tilted her head. "Really? That is odd. No one touched the jumps before your round."

Clara stared at her. Something in Megan's voice felt too smooth. Too easy.

Or maybe Clara was imagining things.

Liam approached next, Knightfall dancing behind him.

"You did what you had to do," Liam said. "If a horse hesitates, breaking rhythm is safer than forcing them. Aspen did not look ready for that line anyway."

Clara's cheeks flushed hot.

"He was ready," she said quietly. "Someone sabotaged the jump."

Liam's brows twitched in mild surprise. "You think someone did it on purpose?"

Clara swallowed. "I think someone touched it."

Liam nodded once. "Well. It was dangerous. Good thing you saw it."

He walked away with Knightfall, who snorted loudly and pawed at the ground.

Clara could not read Liam's expression.

She was not sure she wanted to.

Back at the trailer, Clara removed Aspen's bridle and pressed her forehead against his neck. His breath slowed to a gentle rhythm.

Luke joined her after a few minutes.

"You saved him," he said softly.

Clara shook her head. "He saved himself. I only listened."

"That is exactly why he trusts you," Luke replied.

Clara swallowed, throat tight.

"You are worried," Luke said quietly. "Tell me."

Clara lifted her head. "What if I cannot keep him safe in medal season? What if the pressure gets worse? What if someone is targeting Willowcreek?"

Luke took a slow breath.

"I saw something strange this morning," he admitted. "Poles that had been moved out of place. A groundline shifted during practice. At first I thought it was wind or a mistake by the younger riders. Now I am not so sure."

Clara's heart drummed against her ribs. "So someone is interfering."

Luke shook his head. "I cannot say that yet. Not without proof. But I can say this. You trusted Aspen today. And that trust saved both of you."

Clara stared at Aspen, who chewed hay calmly now.

"I felt so helpless in the ring," she whispered. "I wanted to be brave. But all I felt was fear."

"Fear is not failure," Luke said. "Fear is information. And what you did today was brave. Pulling out was brave. Speaking up was brave. Most riders would have kept going and hoped for luck."

Clara wiped her cheek with the back of her hand. She had not realised a tear had fallen.

"I am tired," she whispered. "Tired of comparing myself. Tired of trying to keep up. Tired of being scared."

Luke rested a hand gently on Aspen's neck.

"You are in the hardest part of the season," he said. "The part where you question everything. But you are not alone. Aspen is with you. I am with you. And this moment, as terrible as it feels, will be the one you look back on later and see as a turning point."

Clara looked up, eyes wet.

"A turning point?"

"Yes," Luke said. "This is where you choose what rider you want to become."

Clara leaned into Aspen and let her breath release.

She wanted to be strong.

She wanted to be capable.

She wanted to protect Aspen.

She wanted to rise.

She just did not know how yet.

But something inside her shifted, like the soft crack of ice beginning to melt.

She whispered into Aspen's mane.

"We will keep going."

Aspen flicked an ear, as if agreeing.

Luke nodded.

"Good," he said. "Because the hardest and most important ride of your season is coming."

Clara frowned. "Which one?"

Luke smiled gently.

"You will know when it arrives."

Clara let out a shaky exhale.

Somewhere across the showgrounds, Megan's laugh rang out. Liam's voice followed, calm and confident. Knightfall snorted loudly.

A storm was building.

But Clara did not yet know that in Chapter 9 she would walk straight into the heart of it.

And come out changed forever.

9

The morning after the dangerous groundline incident arrived quietly, as if the world wanted to apologise for everything it had taken from Clara the day before. A pale, early light rolled gently across Willowcreek, casting long silver ribbons over the paddocks. Mist drifted above the grass like soft breath. The air smelled of pine, creek water, and damp earth.

Clara arrived before anyone else. She stepped out of the truck without the usual rush of nerves, though her heart still held a trembling ache. Something inside her had cracked yesterday. Not broken. Cracked. The kind of crack that lets light in when the world finally slows down enough for the truth to settle.

Aspen stood near the fence, head lowered, tail swishing lazily. He lifted his head the moment he sensed her. His soft nicker drifted through the morning quiet. Then he walked toward her with his gentle, careful steps.

Clara leaned her forehead against his and breathed him in.

"Hi," she whispered. "I did not sleep much."

Aspen brushed his nose along her shoulder. He understood more than people did.

Clara had spent half the night replaying the altered groundline. The panic in Aspen's stride. The sudden halt of the round. The whispers from the crowd. Liam's neutral expression. Megan's calculated curiosity. Luke's calm reassurance.

She had spiraled.

Then numbed.

Then spiraled again.

Until finally, very late, something in her mind whispered truths she had tried to ignore.

She was not riding for herself.

She was riding to keep up.

To impress.

To prove something.

To not fall behind Liam's shadow or Megan's shine.

And in doing so, she had nearly lost herself.

She traced her fingers along Aspen's neck.

"I am sorry," she said softly. "For everything I pushed. For everything I feared. For comparing us to people who do not ride our story."

Aspen released a warm breath into her palm.

Clara exhaled shakily. "I do not want that anymore."

A gentle crunch of gravel behind her made her turn.

Luke approached with two cups of steaming tea. His hair was still damp from a rushed morning shower. His jacket hung open, and he looked as tired as Clara felt.

"You are here early," he said.

"So are you," Clara replied.

He handed her a cup. "You look like you did not sleep."

"I did not."

Luke nodded, understanding without prying. "Walk with me."

Clara followed him toward the far edge of the property. Aspen trailed behind them, nibbling at grass along the way. The rising sun painted the skyline in soft oranges and pinks.

They walked in silence for a few minutes. Luke seemed to be

waiting for her to speak. Clara stared at the field, hands cradling the warm cup.

"Luke," she began quietly. "I think I lost something yesterday."

Luke glanced at her, eyes steady. "What do you mean?"

Clara swallowed. "I lost myself. Or maybe I realised I have been losing myself for a while."

He did not interrupt.

Clara paused near the creek, watching the water ripple. "I keep thinking about how I rode as a kid. Before the pressure. Before shows. I loved it. I ran through fields. I rode bareback. I did not care if anyone watched."

She paused again, her voice almost breaking.

"Now I care about everything. Rankings. Comments. Liam. Megan. Who is faster. Who looks better. Who the judges seem to watch. I care so much about everything that I feel like I am losing the reason I ever wanted this."

Luke took a slow breath. "You have been carrying too many voices."

Clara blinked back tears. "Yes."

"Whose voice is missing?" Luke asked quietly.

Clara stared at the creek.

"My own," she whispered. "And Aspen's."

Aspen nudged her gently, as if to confirm it.

Luke nodded. "Then today is the day you start listening to those again."

Clara closed her eyes for a moment.

"I want to," she said. "I really do."

"Then we will start differently," Luke said. "At sunrise. With no pressure. No jumps. No audience. Just you and him."

Clara hesitated. "A sunrise ride?"

Luke nodded. "You remember what happened last spring. You found yourself in the quiet. You faced fear without force. You rode for courage, not competition."

Clara inhaled sharply. That moment had changed everything.

Luke had found her in the dark, spiraling before her spring show. They had ridden at dawn, side by side, letting the world soften. The quiet had cleared the fog of fear.

Luke looked at her now. "You need that again."

Clara nodded slowly. "Yes. I think so."

They tacked Aspen in the soft golden light of early morning. Clara moved slowly, almost reverently. She brushed Aspen's coat until it gleamed. She checked every buckle twice. She braided his mane loosely, not for presentation, but for the ritual of care. For connection.

She mounted quietly, letting Aspen feel her weight gradually. He shifted under her in familiar comfort.

Luke mounted his grey gelding and moved beside her.

"Ready?" he asked.

Clara nodded.

They headed toward the creek first, letting the horses walk in long, easy strides. The cooling morning air wrapped around Clara like a balm. Birds chirped from somewhere high in the oak trees. The world felt new again.

Luke rode slightly ahead, letting Clara set her own pace.

Aspen's ears flicked forward. His stride stretched. His head lowered into the reins. He breathed deeply through his nostrils, settling into a content rhythm.

Clara exhaled slowly.

"He feels relaxed," she said softly.

"He feels you," Luke replied.

They followed the creek until it curved behind the western pasture. The sun rose steadily behind them, turning the water gold.

Luke glanced over his shoulder. "Pick up a trot when you are ready."

Clara nudged Aspen gently. He moved into a trot with an ease she had not felt since spring. Light. Comfortable. Confident. Clara let the reins slide slightly through her palms, trusting him.

Aspen stretched his neck forward, trotting in long diagonal strides that rolled beneath her seat.

Clara's heart lifted.

Her shoulders softened.

Her breath steadied.

She felt the memories tug at her. Learning to trot at eight years old. Riding bareback at sunset with her hair loose. Whispering secrets to her first pony in the stable. The feeling of freedom that had once been stronger than any fear.

Tears welled in her eyes.

"Are you alright?" Luke asked gently from behind.

Clara nodded and wiped her cheek. "Yes. Better than alright. I remember."

Luke drew closer. "Remember what?"

"Why I love this," Clara whispered.

She slowed Aspen to a walk and let her fingers trail through his mane.

"I have been riding for the wrong reasons," she said. "Trying to prove something. Trying to keep up. Trying not to disappoint anyone."

Luke guided his horse beside hers. "And now?"

"And now," Clara said quietly, "I want to ride for us again."

Luke nodded slowly, a gentle smile forming. "Good."

Clara breathed deeply, the knot in her chest unraveling one slow thread at a time.

"I am scared," she admitted. "Not of jumps. Not of falling. I am scared of losing myself again. Of letting other people decide who I should be."

Luke studied her, thoughtful and calm.

"Clara," he said quietly. "Ride for truth, not applause."

Clara froze.

Her breath caught.

His words sank into her slowly, like sunlight warming the coldest part of her heart.

Ride for truth, not applause.

Clara stared ahead, letting the words echo inside her.

Truth.

Not pressure.

Not comparison.

Not rankings.

Not Megan.

Not Liam.

Not comments online.

Truth.

Aspen walked with a gentle sway beneath her. Clara leaned forward and touched his neck.

"We are doing this our way," she whispered.

Luke rode ahead to give her space, but she could feel his presence like a steady anchor.

Aspen exhaled softly.

Clara smiled.

For the first time in weeks, she felt something solid beneath her fear.

Choice.

Her choice.

Not anyone else's.

And slowly, the sun lifted higher, spilling light across the valley as if blessing her decision.

She would continue the medal season.

Not to win.

Not to impress.

But because she loved riding.

Because she loved Aspen.

Because she wanted to see who she could become when she rode from truth and not expectation.

Clara inhaled deeply, the morning air filling her lungs.

She was ready.
Not for medals.
Not for ribbons.
But for herself.
And that would change everything.

————

The sun had climbed higher by the time Clara and Luke turned back toward Willowcreek. Light spilled across the hills in soft gold, warming the fields and catching in Aspen's mane as he trotted beside her. The morning felt brighter, but Clara felt brighter too. Lighter. Steadier. More herself than she had been in weeks.

They reached the main trail leading back toward the barn. Grass brushed gently against Aspen's fetlocks. Birds hopped along the fence posts. A soft breeze carried the scent of warm hay and distant woodsmoke from a neighbor's farmhouse.

Clara breathed it all in.

Luke slowed his grey to a walk and let Clara pull up alongside him. He studied her for a moment, eyes warm, as if he were taking in the change he saw but would not comment on unless invited.

"Your seat has changed," Luke said finally.

Clara blinked. "Changed how?"

He shrugged lightly. "Relaxed. Not in a collapsed way. In a confident way. A trusting way."

Clara looked down at her posture. Her legs hung long. Her shoulders rested naturally. Her hands were soft on the reins, following Aspen's motion without tension.

"I do feel different," she admitted. "Like the heavy part is starting to melt."

"That is how it works," Luke said. "You do not wake up one day fearless. You wake up just willing to try again."

Clara smiled faintly. "I want to ride like this more. Without noise. Without expectations."

"You can," Luke said. "But you will need boundaries with the people who add pressure."

Clara thought instantly of Megan. And Liam. And the quiet whispers that always seemed to follow her at shows.

"I do not know how to do that," Clara said. "I do not know how to block the noise."

Luke guided his horse around a patch of uneven ground, then looked back toward her.

"You do not block it," he said. "You choose what you let in."

Clara let the words settle.

"You let in what strengthens you," Luke continued. "You shut out what weakens you. It takes practice. But you have already started."

Clara exhaled. "By coming out here?"

Luke shook his head. "By admitting you were scared."

The words struck her deeply.

"I was scared," Clara said softly.

"Of what?" Luke asked.

She hesitated, then replied honestly. "Of losing myself. Of losing Aspen. Of not being enough. Of letting everyone see that I am not as bold as they think I should be."

Luke nodded. "Fear grows quiet when you speak it. It grows loud when you pretend it is not there."

Clara blinked at him. "How do you know all this?"

Luke smiled a little. "Because I have been where you are. Every good rider has."

Clara stared at him, surprised.

"You?" she asked. "You do not seem scared of anything."

Luke laughed softly. "I was terrified for years. Terrified of falling. Terrified of failing. Terrified of disappointing people. Terrified of letting a horse down."

Clara studied his face. "What changed?"

Luke turned his gaze toward the hills, watching the valley wake.

"I finally learned to ride for truth, not applause," he said. "Just like I told you."

Clara felt those words settle into her again. Deeply. Permanently. Truth over applause.

Maybe that was what had pulled her out of bed this morning. Maybe that was what had carried her across the dawn fields. And maybe that was what would carry her through the rest of the season.

Luke nodded toward Aspen. "Let him canter if you want. Let him feel the freedom too."

Clara squeezed gently. Aspen lifted into a smooth canter, his strides rolling like soft waves beneath her. She let her reins slip, trusting him. He carried her forward with a steady rhythm, not fast, not flashy, just sure.

Clara closed her eyes for a moment, feeling the wind brushes across her cheeks.

She remembered the little girl she used to be.

Running barefoot across fields.

Begging her parents to let her stay at the barn longer.

Riding her first pony without a care for angles or distances.

Laughing when she slipped sideways.

Clinging to a mane in pure joy.

That girl lived inside her still.

She had just forgotten how to hear her.

She slowed Aspen to a trot, then a walk, as the barn came into view. Willowcreek stood peaceful in the morning light. Horses grazed. The arena sat empty. The barn cats lounged on the front railing.

Clara felt the difference immediately.

The pressure was gone.

The expectations were quiet.

The noise had faded.

All that remained was the steady beat of Aspen's hoofsteps and the warmth spreading through her chest.

· · ·

When they returned to the yard, Clara dismounted and let Aspen graze while she sat on the fence beside Luke.

The quiet lingered, soft and full.

Then Clara spoke.

"I want to keep riding the medal season," she said softly. "Not because I want to beat Liam. Not because I want Megan to stop talking. Not because I want judges to notice me."

Luke nodded, encouraging her to continue.

"Because I want to know what I can do," Clara said. "Who I can be. I want to see what happens when I ride the way I did today. Honestly. Fearfully. Brave anyway."

Luke smiled quietly. "That is the decision I was hoping for."

Tears pricked at Clara's eyes. "Really?"

"Yes," Luke said. "Because quitting out of fear is one thing. Choosing to step forward even when you are scared is something else entirely."

Clara looked down at her hands.

"I do not want to be controlled by fear anymore."

"And you will not be," Luke said simply. "Not after today."

Clara inhaled slowly. She felt her spine lengthen, her shoulders rise, her breath deepen.

"I want to train differently," she said. "Not harder. Not faster. Just differently."

"What do you have in mind?" Luke asked.

Clara thought for a moment. "More quiet rides. More connection. More understanding between me and Aspen. Less pressure to be perfect. More rides like today. More truth."

Luke nodded approvingly. "That is exactly what I hoped you would say."

Clara laughed softly. "Were you waiting for me to figure it out?"

Luke shrugged. "Growth cannot be forced. It can only be supported."

Clara looked at him with a warm, grateful expression. "Thank you. For everything. For letting me crack without breaking."

"You did not crack," Luke corrected. "You shed what was holding you too tightly."

Clara felt her throat tighten again.

He stood. "Walk Aspen out. Let him roll. Then go home. Rest. Tomorrow, we begin the kind of training that honors who you truly are."

Clara nodded. "I am ready."

And to her surprise, she truly meant it.

Aspen followed her to the paddock, his ears flicking happily. Clara unclipped the lead rope and stepped back.

Aspen lowered his head, sniffed the ground, and then dropped into a deep, exuberant roll. Dirt and dust flew into the air, sparkling in the sunlight. Clara laughed. She could not remember the last time she found pure joy in that simple sight.

Aspen rolled once, twice, then leaped back to his feet, shaking vigorously. Clara clapped her hands once in delight.

"You look ridiculous," she said.

He snorted proudly.

She walked over and pressed her forehead to his shoulder. His warmth filled her. His steady heartbeat anchored her.

"We are doing this our way," she whispered. "Win or lose, we will ride the truth. Not the noise."

Aspen breathed deeply, as if taking her words into himself.

Clara stepped back and watched him trot across the paddock with bright, eager steps. He looked free. He looked confident. He looked like himself.

For the first time in a long time, so did she.

As Clara headed back toward the truck, Jenna caught sight of her and jogged over, slightly out of breath.

"Hey," Jenna said. "Are you alright? I heard about yesterday.

Someone said Aspen refused. Someone else said the jump was messed up. And Megan said…"

Clara held up a hand gently.

"Jenna," she said softly. "It is alright. I am okay. Aspen is okay. And… I am figuring things out."

Jenna studied her for a moment. "You look different today. Happier. Or lighter."

Clara smiled. "Both."

Jenna tilted her head. "Does that mean you are staying in medal season?"

"Yes," Clara said. The word came easily now. "But I am doing it differently."

Jenna grinned. "Good. Because I cannot face Megan on my own."

Clara laughed. "You will not."

Jenna bumped her shoulder playfully. "Good. Then let us both survive this season."

"We will," Clara said.

And she believed it.

Later that afternoon, Clara returned to Willowcreek for Aspen's evening check. The barn was quiet again. A few riders groomed their horses in peaceful silence. Liam had left earlier. Megan had taken Evermore on a hack with two senior riders. The chaotic energy from the day before was gone.

Clara walked to Aspen's paddock, leaning on the fence as he grazed in the soft evening light.

She called softly. "Aspen."

He lifted his head, ears alert, eyes bright.

Clara smiled and whispered, "Thank you. For trying. For trusting. For waiting for me to come back to myself."

He walked toward her and pressed his muzzle gently into her palm.

Clara closed her eyes.

This.

This moment.

This connection.

This truth.

This was why she rode.

Not medals.

Not applause.

Not comments online.

Just this.

She felt a soft certainty settle into her heart, like water finding its home.

She was ready.

Ready to ride for truth.

Ready to ride for courage.

Ready to ride for herself.

Ready to ride for Aspen.

Whatever happened next, she would face it with a steady hand and a braver heart.

And in the days ahead, when the storm finally broke for real, she would need that courage more than she ever knew.

But for now, Clara stood beside Aspen in the quiet evening light and felt her courage return like dawn over the valley.

10

The air felt strange that morning. Heavy. Electric. Almost humming with an invisible pressure that made Clara's skin prickle before she even left the truck. The sky was a pale steel grey, thin clouds stretched across the horizon like pulled cotton. It was not quite rain. Not quite wind. But something between.

Aspen pawed anxiously at the dirt near the trailer, lifting his head quickly whenever a horse moved nearby. Clara stroked his cheek, trying to calm him, but he felt different today. His energy sat close to the surface, restless and unsettled.

Luke arrived moments later, carrying the tack trunk with one hand, a thermos of coffee in the other. He paused beside Clara, eyes scanning the grounds with a trainer's instinct that picked up things most people dismissed.

"Crowded," he murmured.

It was crowded. More barns than usual. More spectators. More trainers. More tension. The medal qualifiers always brought pressure, but today the pressure felt alive.

Clara tightened Aspen's girth, her breath steady but her heart uneasy.

"Do you feel it too?" she whispered.

Aspen flicked his ears back and forth. That was answer enough.

The warm up ring was already a storm in motion.

Horses surged past each other. Riders called warnings that went ignored. Trainers raised jumps too quickly, lowered them too late. Poles rattled. Someone dropped a whip. A horse bucked. A pony squealed. Dogs barked along the rail. Spectators pressed in too close.

Clara's throat tightened the moment she stepped inside.

Aspen, already tense, curled his neck and danced sideways. His breathing came faster, nostrils flaring with each step.

"Easy," Clara said, voice low. "I am right here."

But he did not soften.

Not today.

Luke was already watching closely. "Stay along the outside track. No jumping until he settles. Let him move forward. Do not hold him too tightly."

Clara nodded and eased Aspen along the rail. His stride remained tight, stiff, uncertain. He tossed his head and shied when a chestnut mare bolted across the arena.

Clara steadied him with gentle hands. "It is alright. We are alright."

But she was not sure she believed it.

They warmed up for several minutes. Moments of calm flickered through the chaos, but never lasted. Someone shouted. Someone dropped a pole. Knightfall reared in the far corner. A rider fell. Trainers rushed in.

Clara flinched at every loud sound. Aspen felt each flinch and reacted with nervous steps.

Luke approached the rail. "Do not let the ring steal your breath. Breathe for him."

Clara inhaled deeply, steadying her trembling hands.

"Again," Luke said. "Slow. Deep."

She obeyed. Aspen responded a little, lowering his head by an inch.

Liam and Knightfall entered just then, casting a sharp ripple through the atmosphere. Knightfall snorted loudly, hooves striking the sand like thunder. His muscles bunched and released in restless waves. Liam guided him with firm hands, posture perfect, calm as always, but Knightfall's agitation seeped into the air like static.

Aspen felt it instantly.

He jolted forward, almost into another rider.

Clara pulled him back, heart hammering. "Easy. Please, easy."

Megan trotted past, Evermore shining under his polished tack. She tossed her hair and smiled at Liam.

"Warm up looks wild today," she said.

Liam nodded. "Good pressure training."

Clara bit the inside of her cheek. Heat flushed up her neck.

Luke saw the tension building and moved quickly to Clara's side.

"Clara," he said quietly. "Stay in your lane. Do not look at them. Focus on your horse."

Clara nodded. "I am trying."

"I know," Luke said. "Keep going."

The steward raised the warm up oxer at the center of the ring. Riders lined up. The pressure grew.

Clara did not want to go near the jump yet, but Aspen kept tossing his head, feeding off the tension of the ring. He needed something to focus on. Something steady.

She decided on one small vertical, just to give him direction.

A Knightfall rider cut her off before she reached it.

Aspen sidestepped sharply.

Clara steadied him. "We will try again."

She circled.

Liam turned Knightfall toward the same vertical, his trajectory too close for comfort. Clara hesitated, then shifted away.

Liam cleared the jump effortlessly, Knightfall landing in a burst of power.

Clara circled again. She approached the jump at a quiet trot.

This time, just as Aspen lifted his front feet, a rider behind her shouted, "Inside line!"

Clara did not have space to yield.

Aspen jumped crookedly, landing on the wrong lead, scrambling for balance.

Clara sat deep, holding him steady until he recovered.

Luke called sharply from the rail, "Everyone pays attention. It is too tight in here. Keep distance or get out."

No one listened.

The ring grew hotter, tighter, louder.

Clara's nerves stretched thinner.

Aspen's nerves stretched even thinner.

The steward raised the oxer again. Knightfall surged toward it, snorting and shaking his head.

Aspen froze.

His body locked beneath Clara.

"Hey," Clara whispered. "Breathe with me."

She inhaled deeply.

Aspen did not.

He trembled.

Knightfall took the oxer in a powerful leap, landing so close that his tail brushed Aspen's flank.

Aspen exploded.

Not bucking. Not rearing. Exploded in fear. He spun sideways, scrambling, hooves skidding in the churned sand. Clara grabbed his mane, steadying herself as the world tilted around them.

Luke shouted, "Clara, disengage him. Bend. Bend."

Clara acted instantly, flexing him into a small circle, breathing in sharp, steady bursts.

Aspen fought it for a moment, then slowed, trembling violently.

Clara's own hands shook.

Megan approached, breathless with excitement instead of concern.

"Wow," she said. "That was close. Knightfall is on fire today."

Clara stared at her. "Aspen nearly fell."

Megan shrugged. "He is sensitive. Liam and Knightfall cannot be expected to stay tiny just because he gets rattled."

Clara felt heat burn behind her eyes.

Jenna trotted up, face pale. "Clara, do you want to step out? I can get Luke."

"No," Clara said, voice shaky but firm. "We will try again."

"Are you sure?"

"Yes," Clara whispered. "He needs to know we are okay."

Aspen snorted hard, foam forming at the corners of his mouth.

Luke approached again, calm but concerned. "You can step out if you need to."

Clara shook her head. "If I leave now, he will stay scared. If I stay, we might work through it."

Luke studied her for a moment, then nodded. "Then stay. But stay smart. No more jumping until he settles."

Clara stroked Aspen's neck, whispering to him.

"We are safe. I promise."

The ring surged again. A horse refused a jump loudly. A pole crashed to the ground. Someone cursed. Someone told someone else to move. Knightfall powered past, blowing hot breath and shaking sweat into the air.

Aspen jolted.

Clara steadied him.

He jolted again.

Clara softened the reins.

He hopped sideways, terrified.

Clara breathed with him, patient, steady.

"Look at me," she whispered. "I am here."

Aspen flicked an ear, just one, but enough to tell her he heard her.

She circled him again, keeping her posture calm even while her heart pounded wildly.

Luke watched, stepping closer when needed, stepping back when she found a moment of rhythm.

Minutes passed. The chaos persisted.

But slowly, Aspen's breathing changed.

Slow exhales.

Soft releases.

Neck lowering an inch.

Then another.

His stride untangled itself.

Clara felt her lungs loosen too.

"Good boy," she whispered. "You are so brave."

Liam rode past them, Knightfall held in a tight, collected canter.

"You staying in?" he asked.

Clara nodded. "Yes."

"You sure?"

"Yes," she said, stronger this time.

Knightfall snorted and tossed his head. Liam continued on.

Aspen kept his ears on Clara now, not Knightfall.

Progress.

Then Megan rode by and said, "Your round is soon. I hope Aspen finds his courage by then."

But for the first time in weeks, Clara did not flinch at Megan's words.

Because Aspen lifted his head and touched her boot with his nose, seeking direction from her and no one else.

Courage was not loud.

Courage was not flashy.

Courage was steady.

Courage was quiet.

Courage was small steps in the middle of chaos.

And that was what she and Aspen had found.

. . .

Their round was called.

Clara exhaled once, long and controlled.

She did not check Megan.

She did not check Liam.

She did not check the spectators.

She did not check the judges.

She checked Aspen.

He looked back at her with bright, uncertain eyes, but his breathing was steady now. His weight was evenly balanced. His ears flicked toward the course.

Clara stroked his neck. "We will go together. That is all."

Luke stepped beside her stirrup as she gathered the reins.

"You handled that storm," he said quietly. "Now ride the calm that follows."

Clara smiled faintly. "We will try."

Luke nodded. "Ride for truth."

Clara felt her heart swell.

"Not applause," she whispered.

"Exactly."

They entered the ring.

Clara's hands were no longer shaking.

Aspen's steps were no longer scattered.

The chaos of the warm up was behind them.

The storm was behind them.

And ahead, for the first time in a long time, Clara saw only their journey.

Aspen trotted forward softly, ears pricked.

Clara breathed once.

They began their course.

11

Clara guided Aspen toward the out gate after their stormy warm up victory and their steady, heart led round. Her hands still tingled from the effort of riding with every ounce of honesty she possessed. Her lungs felt open again. Her heartbeat steadied, although the adrenaline continued to pulse gently through her body.

Aspen's ears twitched forward and back, but the frantic tension from earlier was gone. His stride carried a softness that only came when he felt safe. When he felt understood. When he felt anchored to her.

As they left the ring, applause broke out. Not loud. But warm. Genuine. Supportive.

Clara blinked in surprise.

Jenna rushed up to the rail, eyes bright. "Clara, that was beautiful. You did not chase perfection. You rode with heart."

Clara's throat tightened. "Thank you."

"You changed today," Jenna said. "I do not know what happened this morning, but you are riding differently. I can see it."

Clara smiled softly. "I finally remembered why I love this."

Jenna squeezed her hand quickly before running back to help another rider.

Clara walked Aspen toward the cool down area, letting the reins slide long. She wanted to feel every breath he took. Every step. Every tiny sign that he was still with her. The breeze brushed her cheeks and carried whispers from the crowd.

"That bay mare was good."

"The stallion was wild."

"Did you see the chestnut? Sensitive, but what a try."

"Clara Bennett. Yes, she rode beautifully."

Clara swallowed hard, overwhelmed.

Applause no longer twisted her chest.

Today it felt like kindness, not pressure.

Luke met her at the far end, stepping forward with quiet pride. He placed his hand on Aspen's neck first, giving the gelding a long, slow stroke.

"Well done," he said softly.

Clara looked at him, fighting the sting in her eyes. "Thank you. For everything. I almost lost myself this season."

Luke shook his head gently. "You did not lose yourself. You stepped away from noise long enough to hear who you truly are."

Clara laughed quietly. "You always know what to say."

"That is my job," Luke replied. "But it is also true."

Aspen lowered his head to sniff Luke's boot. Luke scratched his chin.

"And him," Luke added, "he is carrying you with so much honesty. Sensitive horses are not a weakness. They teach you to ride with grace instead of control."

Clara ran her fingers through Aspen's mane. "He is my heart."

Luke nodded. "Then trust him. And trust yourself. The rest will fall into place."

. . .

They walked Aspen to the wash rack. Cool water streamed over his legs, his back, his shoulders. He sighed deeply, leaning slightly into Clara's touch. His muscles relaxed, taking the morning's tension with them.

Clara rested her forehead against his neck and whispered, "You were amazing."

A quiet sound behind her made her turn.

Megan stood there, Evermore at her side. Her helmet was off, revealing damp hair pinned behind her ears. For once, her expression was not competing or gloating.

She looked hesitant.

Clara blinked. "Hi."

Megan shifted awkwardly. "I saw your round."

Clara's stomach tightened out of habit, expecting critique or comparison.

But Megan said something entirely unexpected.

"It was brave," she said quietly. "Not in the flashy way. In the real way."

Clara's breath caught.

Megan glanced at Aspen. "Sometimes horses like him get overwhelmed. Most riders push harder when they should listen. You did not."

Her voice cracked slightly. Clara noticed.

"Megan," Clara said softly, "are you okay?"

For a moment, Megan's guard slipped.

Just for a moment.

And beneath it Clara saw something she had never expected.

Fear.

Pressure.

Loneliness.

Megan swallowed. "It is nothing."

"It is not nothing," Clara said gently. "Tell me."

Megan looked away, as if considering running from the conversation. Then her shoulders sagged.

"Everyone thinks Evermore and I have everything together," she whispered. "Perfect pair. Perfect image. Perfect rounds."

Clara nodded silently.

"But it is a lie," Megan continued. "He is brilliant, but he is difficult too. He gets hot. He gets anxious. And I... I get scared to admit it because I am expected to be strong. Perfect. Confident."

Clara's heart lifted in a new, surprising ache.

Megan's voice grew quiet. "Evermore spooked in our warm up today. Twice. And I pretended he did not. I pretended I did not. But inside I was panicking."

Clara stepped closer. "You could have told someone."

Megan shook her head. "No. My trainer expects perfection. My parents expect results. And Liam... well, Liam sees everyone as competition."

Clara frowned. "Liam is intense, but he is not unkind."

"He is not cruel," Megan agreed. "But he thrives in pressure. I do not. Not like he does. He thinks fear makes people weak."

Clara felt her stomach twist. "Fear does not make anyone weak."

Megan let out a shaky breath. "I wish everyone thought like you."

Something shifted between them. Not friendship. Not yet. But the beginning of understanding. The beginning of seeing each other not as rivals but as people riding their own battles.

Clara reached out and touched Megan's arm lightly. "It is alright to be scared. It is alright to ask for help."

Megan blinked hard. "You mean that?"

"Yes," Clara said. "We are all just trying."

Megan nodded slowly and whispered, "Thank you."

Evermore nudged her shoulder, breaking the tension.

Megan took a breath and straightened. "Good luck in your next round. Not that you need it."

Clara smiled, genuine and warm. "Thanks. You too."

Megan nodded and led Evermore away, her posture softer than before.

Clara watched her go and felt something she never expected.
Empathy.
Not competition.
Empathy.

Later, Clara walked Aspen toward a grassy hill behind the showgrounds. The wind picked up, lifting strands of her hair. A storm cloud gathered on the horizon, but the sky above them remained clear.

Clara sat on the hill, Aspen grazing quietly beside her.
She replayed the morning.
The fear.
The storm.
The chaos.
The near collision.
Aspen's panic.
Her panic.
The moment she breathed with him anyway.
Her round.
The applause.
Luke's words.
Megan's unmasked vulnerability.
She felt something inside her settle.
She was not chasing medals anymore.
She was not chasing rankings.
She was not chasing approval.
She was chasing truth.
Courage.
Her voice.
Aspen's trust.
And the feeling that came when she rode for something other than applause.

Clara pressed her hand to her chest.

Her heartbeat was strong.

Steady.

Sure.

Aspen lifted his head and walked to her, inviting her back into the moment.

She stood and wrapped her arms around his neck.

"No matter what happens," she whispered, "I will ride for us."

Aspen breathed into her hair.

A familiar voice approached behind them.

Liam.

"Your round was solid," he said.

Clara turned slowly. Liam stood with Knightfall, the stallion snorting and pawing at the ground. Liam's expression was neutral, unreadable.

"Thanks," Clara said quietly.

"I saw the warm up," Liam said. "Knightfall was difficult today. I could barely hold him. But Aspen stayed with you."

Clara nodded.

Liam continued, almost reluctantly. "You handled it well."

Clara blinked in surprise. "Thank you."

"You are different from most riders," Liam said. "You are not scared of the truth."

Clara tilted her head. "Are you?"

Liam looked away. "Knightfall is a brilliant horse. But he is a lot. Some days I pretend I can control him. Some days I pretend he does not scare me."

Clara waited.

Liam inhaled deeply. "Today he scared me."

Clara softened. "You do not have to pretend."

He met her eyes, and something unspoken passed between them.

Not romance.

Not rivalry.

Just honest recognition.

Two riders who had faced storms and found cracks in their armor.

Liam nodded once and led Knightfall away.

As the afternoon sun dipped low, Willowcreek's riders gathered near the ring for the final tallies of the day. Jenna stood beside Clara. Lara beside her. Megan a few feet away. Liam on the opposite end. Luke in the center, a calm anchor.

Scores for the day scrolled across the board.

Clara placed in the middle.

Megan placed higher.

Liam placed highest.

But Clara felt no sting. No jealousy. No panic.

Just clarity.

When Luke stepped beside her, he nodded.

"You found your truth today," he said.

"And my courage," Clara replied.

Luke smiled gently. "The season is not over. But your direction is clear now."

Clara looked at Aspen, his copper coat gleaming in the fading light.

"As long as he is beside me," she said, "I can face anything."

Luke nodded. "Then you are ready for the final chapter."

Clara breathed deeply.

She believed him.

Winter was coming.

A clinic invitation awaited.

Her journey was not done.

Not even close.

But for the first time in a long time, Clara felt grounded in herself.

Ready.

Steady.

True.

And as the sun set behind the hills, she whispered into Aspen's mane:

"Whatever comes next, we ride together."

12

The last qualifier ended under a sky washed clean by evening light. The crowds thinned gradually, drifting toward trailers and warm cars. Dust settled over the arena in soft golden layers. In the quiet that came after the chaos, Clara led Aspen along the fence line, letting him stretch his neck in long, easy steps.

She did not know what her score was yet.

She did not care.

Not today.

Her round had been steady, honest, and full of heart. Aspen had trusted her. She had trusted him. There was no shaking that feeling. No comparing it. No watering it down.

Luke walked beside her with a calm expression, his hands tucked loosely into the pockets of his coat. His steps matched hers without effort, as if this slow walk after a long day had become part of their unspoken routine.

Jenna jogged up breathlessly. "Clara, they want you at the judge's tent. Something about... well, something important."

Clara blinked. "Me?"

"Yes," Jenna said. "You should go. Luke, go with her."

Luke nodded and turned toward Clara. "Let us find out."

They walked toward the small white tent at the far corner of the showground. Trainers milled around. A few riders lingered nearby, whispering among themselves. As Clara approached, Amber Leigh emerged from the tent. Her posture was elegant as always. Her jacket was crisp. Her eyes sharp.

Behind her, Liam stood holding Knightfall's reins. He looked calm but watchful, studying Clara with that unreadable intensity she had come to recognize.

Amber stepped forward.

"Clara," she said, voice smooth. "I watched your round."

Clara swallowed lightly. "Thank you."

Amber nodded. "I watched your warm up too."

The comment hung heavily for a moment. Clara did not know if Amber meant that as praise or concern.

Amber continued, folding her hands. "Knightfall Equestrian Center will be opening four apprenticeship slots this winter for young riders with potential. These positions are rare. Demanding. And they are stepping stones to higher levels of competition."

Clara's breath hitched.

Amber held her gaze. "Liam is one of our strongest riders. But we need more like him. Disciplined. Self aware. Driven. Today you showed qualities that matter deeply to us. You stayed calm under pressure. You protected your horse. You made brave choices. And you rode with honesty."

Clara could not speak.

Amber continued. "I would like you to consider joining Knightfall this winter. Full training. Full schedule. Elite coaching. You would leave Willowcreek for the season."

Clara felt the world shift slightly beneath her feet.

Behind Amber, Liam's expression flickered in something that might have been approval. Or warning. Or a mixture of both.

Amber stepped closer. "Think carefully. Opportunities like this change careers."

Clara finally found her voice. "Thank you. I... I am honored."

"Good," Amber said. "You have until tomorrow evening to decide. Speak with your trainer. Speak with your family. And speak honestly with yourself."

Amber signaled to Liam. He stepped forward slightly.

"Knightfall needs riders who can handle pressure," he said quietly. "You proved that today."

Clara nodded, unsure what to say.

Amber turned sharply, already done with the conversation. Liam followed. Knightfall snorted, pawing at the ground, his dark coat gleaming as they left.

Luke had not spoken once.

Only after they were gone did he finally turn to Clara.

"Are you alright?" he asked gently.

Clara stared at the ground. "I do not know."

Luke nodded slowly. "Let us walk."

They took Aspen toward a quiet corner behind the arena where the noise softened into gentle evening hums. Willow trees swayed in the breeze. Birds chirped from the hedges. The sky shifted into late gold.

Clara stroked Aspen's neck, trying to steady her breathing.

"Knightfall," she whispered. "Amber Leigh. Elite training. Real competition. It is everything riders dream of."

Luke waited.

Clara swallowed. "It could change my whole path. It is powerful. Prestigious. Important."

Luke nodded once. "And?"

Clara squeezed Aspen's reins lightly. "...And terrifying."

Luke's voice was calm. "What scares you?"

She exhaled. "Leaving Willowcreek. Leaving everything that makes me feel grounded. Leaving Aspen's home. Leaving... you."

Luke looked away briefly, then back at her. "You would learn a lot at Knightfall. There is no denying that."

Clara nodded. "I know. And part of me feels like I should want it."

Luke's voice lowered. "Do you want it?"

Clara did not answer immediately.

She thought of Knightfall.

A powerful, brilliant horse.

A storm in motion.

Nothing like Aspen.

She thought of Liam.

Precise.

Disciplined.

Relentless.

Driven by pressure, not peace.

She thought of Amber Leigh.

Cold.

Sharp.

Demanding.

Expecting perfection.

And then she thought of Willowcreek.

Soft mornings.

Quiet hacks.

Luke's steady guidance.

Jenna's chatter.

The barn cats sleeping in the hay.

Warm laughter in the tack room.

Aspen's gentle whinny whenever she arrived.

Her heart knew the truth before her mind caught up.

Clara whispered, "I do not want to ride someone else's future. I want to ride my own."

Luke's shoulders softened. "Then choose the path that feels like yours."

Clara looked at Aspen. His warm eyes reflected everything she needed to remember. The rides that saved her. The fears she faced. The truth she found. The courage she built.

She placed both hands on his face. "Aspen is my horse. My partner. My place in the world."

Luke nodded. "Then trust that."

Clara breathed in deeply, letting the decision settle.

"I am staying," she whispered. "I am choosing Willowcreek."

She felt something inside her unlock. A weight lifted. She had not just chosen a stable. She had chosen herself.

The next morning, Clara returned to the showground before anyone else. Amber Leigh stood near the judge's tent reviewing paperwork, her posture straight as a blade. Liam stood beside Knightfall, adjusting the reins.

Clara approached, steady but respectful.

Amber looked up. "Clara."

"Hi," Clara said softly. "Thank you again for the offer."

Amber waited, expression unreadable.

Clara inhaled slowly. "After thinking carefully... I am honored you considered me. Truly. But I need to follow the path that feels right for me."

Amber's eyes narrowed slightly. "Which is?"

"Willowcreek," Clara said. "My horse. My barn family. The kind of riding that lets me grow honestly. I am grateful for your belief in me. But I am not ready to become a different version of myself just to fit your program."

Amber's face remained composed, but something flickered behind her eyes. Not anger. Something closer to respect.

"You are choosing the quieter path," Amber said.

Clara nodded. "Yes. Because it is mine."

Amber studied her for a moment.

"You are young," she said. "You could go far. Most riders would leap at this opportunity."

Clara smiled softly. "Most riders are not me."

A very small smile touched the corner of Amber's mouth. "It takes conviction to decline something like this."

"It takes understanding," Clara said. "And I finally understand who I am."

Amber nodded once. "Very well. I am disappointed. But I am also impressed. Perhaps more impressed than if you had accepted."

Clara blinked in surprise.

"Few riders have the clarity to choose the right road, not the loud one," Amber said quietly.

She extended her hand.

Clara shook it.

Amber turned and walked away.

Liam remained. He held Knightfall with a firm grip, the stallion tossing his head as if annoyed by the stillness.

Liam stepped closer.

"You said no," he said quietly.

Clara nodded.

His voice softened. "You earned my respect."

Clara blinked. "Thank you."

"Most riders chase prestige," Liam continued. "They chase titles. They chase people's attention. You chase truth. It is rare."

Clara did not know how to respond.

Liam looked at Aspen grazing nearby. "That horse trusts you more than any rider I have ever seen trust a horse. Do not ever forget that."

Clara smiled gently. "I will not."

Liam nodded and mounted Knightfall. The stallion surged forward with restless power, and together they disappeared into the far end of the showground.

Megan approached next, her expression guarded but softer than usual.

She did not say anything at first.

She just nodded.

Clara nodded back.

The gesture was small.

But it was more than they had ever shared.

Understanding.

Peace.

Respect.

Megan whispered, "Good choice."

Clara's eyes warmed. "Thank you."

Then Megan walked away to join Evermore, leaving Clara in the quiet glow of morning.

That evening, Clara tacked up Aspen for one last ride before heading home. She did not choose the arena. She did not choose the pastures.

She chose the creek.

The place where everything had begun.

The place that had healed her winter fears.

The place where she rediscovered her courage in spring.

The place where summer had pushed her to her brink.

They walked in silence, the fading sun brushing gold across Aspen's coat. The water flowed gently beside them, whispering against the stones. Dragonflies skimmed across the surface. The smell of warm grass and drifting pine followed them down the trail.

Clara let Aspen choose the pace. He walked with a steady rhythm, ears flicking forward, relaxed and confident. Her legs rested long at his sides. Her hands held the reins loose and trusting.

She breathed deeply.

This.

This was who she was.

Not the girl who chased applause.

Not the rider who compared herself to others.

Not the young woman afraid of failing.

Clara Bennett.

Aspen's partner.

A rider who had learned to hear herself again.

And to trust who she found.

When they reached the wide bend of Willow Creek, Clara halted and let Aspen drink from the cool water. She leaned forward, stroking his neck in slow circles.

"This trilogy," she whispered, "was never about winning."

Her voice softened, steady and sure.

"It was about becoming someone I could trust."

Aspen lifted his head and flicked his ears toward her, water dripping from his muzzle.

Clara sat tall in the saddle, looking at the path ahead. The creek shimmered. The evening air hummed softly around them. The world felt open again. Honest.

She nudged Aspen lightly.

He stepped forward into the golden light.

Clara breathed one last truth into the quiet valley.

"Whatever comes next, I know who I am in the saddle."

The creek glimmered beside them.

Aspen flicked his ears.

And together they moved into the next season of their life.

Strong.

Steady.

Whole.

The End of the Willowcreek Seasons Trilogy

CLARA'S NOTES TO HERSELF

These are the small reminders I keep for the days when the barn is loud, or my heart feels too full, or I forget why I ride. They live folded inside my tack trunk. Creased. Soft. Honest.

- Breathe until your hands soften.
  - Pressure passes.
  - Ride the horse you have today.
  - Trust takes time.
  - Progress is a quiet story.
  - Courage is choosing to try again.
  - Horses listen to your heartbeat more than your heels.
  - You grow in the slow moments, not the perfect ones.
  - A steady ride is worth more than a flawless one.
  - Look for the softness in every stride.
  - Rest is not quitting.
  - You do not have to be fearless to be brave.
  - Aspen believes in you. Believe in him too.
  - Ride for truth.
  - Ride for joy.

• Ride for the person you are becoming.

And when doubt settles in your chest, remember this:
    You have already faced storms and found your way through.
    You know who you are in the saddle.
    Carry that with you.
    Always.

www.ingramcontent.com/pod-product-compliance
Lightning Source LLC
Chambersburg PA
CBHW071834190726
48292CB00005B/1772